First edition December 2024

ISBN   979-8-9921513-0-5   (paperback)
ISBN   979-8-9921513-1-2   (ebook)

MARSVILLE

by Sarah Zee

One

Cynde slipped out of her babydoll pajamas and dressed in a fitted white t-shirt and a wavy, floral print miniskirt. She laced up her combat boots then sat on her bed, waiting for her mother to come braid her hair.

"Ma, I'm gonna be late!"

She waited another minute then stood to look herself over in the full-length mirror on the back of her bedroom door, running her hands over her flat stomach. She was turning to study her profile when the door opened.

"If you wanna be my lover…" her mother sang mockingly, swiveling her hips around. She was dressed for work in a maroon skirt and blazer set with heels.

"No one even likes the Spice Girls anymore."

"Maybe not, but you sure like to dress like them. You're going to get sent home for that skirt, babes."

"Whatever."

"Not whatever. If you don't start taking school more seriously, you won't get into a good college."

"I don't care."

"You better care. I know it seems like you've got plenty of time, Cynde, but it goes faster than you think. You want choices in life," her mother said, moving behind her, resting her hands on Cynde's shoulders. She looked into the mirror at her daughter. "Stay focused," she said in Cynde's ear. "You're a smart girl with a bright future."

Cynde continued examining her reflection.

"French braids?" her mother asked.

"Uh-huh. Pigtails," she responded, sitting on her bed.

Her mother went to work, neatly braiding Cynde's long, thick, dark hair.

"I want you to go directly to school today. No skipping. I have to work late. I'll leave money for a pizza. And wear a jacket. Your new denim one is on the kitchen table where you left it."

***

The late bell rang just as Cynde made her way through the front entrance. She walked to the girls' bathroom in B hall.

"Hey, Cyn! Cool skirt!"

"Awww, Cynde...your hair is so cute. Mine's too thin. Braids just look dumb on me."

"Hey," Cynde responded simply to the girls huddled at the mirror, studying her own reflection as she smoothed on a coat of cherry lip gloss.

"Are you and Justin going to Spring Fling, Cynde?" someone asked.

"Oh, my God, Cynde, your eyes are so pretty," someone else said.

Cynde often received compliments on her looks. She was slender, but over the past year and a half, she'd developed some noticeable curves. Her hair was silky and, but for a few tiny freckles scattered across the bridge of her nose, her fair complexion was flawless. Her eyes always seemed to attract the most attention though. They were uncommonly large and a vibrant shade of teal.

Cynde knew the other girls envied her, and she knew she was attractive to boys. But last semester, Paul Shale, a junior from her biology class had called her "alien face," and since then, she had wondered if her eyes were perhaps just a bit too large for her face. Or maybe her nose was a touch too narrow, or her mouth too small. She hated that she'd even given Paul's words a second thought. Paul was a nobody—trash from the Manor. Why should she care what he thought? But she did wonder sometimes if perhaps her chin *was* a bit pointy.

Fuck you, Manor boy.

Unintentionally ignoring the girls, she turned away from the mirror, leaving the bathroom, and started toward homeroom. She barely heard her homeroom teacher's lecture about tardiness. Sitting alone at the back of the classroom, she ignored the other students as they stood for the Pledge of Allegiance, instead reading over her notes for first period.

When the bell rang, she headed off to history. Cynde had always hated history before this year. This year, history was taught by Mr. Bauer. He was an unusually tall man with big broad shoulders. He had close cut dark hair that was turning silver just at his temples. Some days, his cleft chin would be covered in just a faint mix of dark and silvery stubble.

Mr. Bauer often entertained the class with stories of his childhood. He'd come from a farming family in Nebraska and had grown up milking cows and husking corn.

3

"These hands...," he would say proudly, holding up his strong hands for them. *"Three hundred ears in 80 minutes."*

Cynde had been to New York City on countless shopping sprees with her mother, followed by dinner at Lutece or Le Grenouille, her mother's two favorite restaurants. Her mother had also taken her on a three-week trip to Paris when she was 13. But otherwise, she had seldom left her tiny suburban hometown of Morrisville, Pennsylvania. She had certainly never been to Nebraska or anywhere else outside of the Mid-Atlantic Region. She'd only ever seen cornfields from the passenger window of a moving vehicle.

But Cynde liked to think about Mr. Bauer on his family's farm in Nebraska, his big strong hands fast at work, running over ear after ear of corn. Sometimes, she'd sit at her desk, staring up at his hands while he lectured. They looked rough, reddish with white and yellow patches of dry broken skin on some of the inner parts of his fingers. Whenever he walked around the classroom to return graded tests, Cynde hoped he would allow his hand to brush against hers. But he never did.

Mr. Bauer was passionate about American history. He liked to talk about the Dust Bowl. Cynde enjoyed watching his face grow serious. The two wrinkles between his silvery black eyebrows would deepen, his eyes narrowing. Sometimes, his jaw would clench just a bit. She liked listening to his voice grow deeper, sounding almost like a soft growl at times.

"There's a right way and a wrong way to do everything on a farm," he'd say, pointing a thick, callused finger at them. *"When the government starts throwing money at farmers to get them to do things the wrong way, there's gonna be trouble."*

Mr. Bauer the farmer.

Mr. Bauer always carried a pack of Marlboro in his shirt pocket and after class, Cynde would follow him outside, and she could usually talk him into letting her bum a cigarette. She didn't really enjoy smoking. It always made her feel just a little bit sick. But she'd learned to inhale without coughing just so she'd have an excuse to talk to Mr. Bauer.

He used to spend that time telling Cynde what a smart girl she was, encouraging her to try harder, to bring up her grades. Early into the school year, she had done just that. She always managed to get an A in history now. Mr. Bauer had made it interesting. Plus, she'd never want to disappoint him.

Only now, Mr. Bauer never told Cynde she was a smart girl anymore. He never talked about her at all anymore—only about history or the upcoming school schedule. He didn't even really seem to look at her; just stood there, smoking and staring up at the sky.

She was just following Mr. Bauer down the hall to see if she could bum a cigarette when Justin called out to her.

"Hey, Cyn!"

She spun and offered a quick wave, continuing after Mr. Bauer.

"Cynde!" Justin called out again. "Hey, com'ere!"

Mr. Bauer stopped and turned to look at Justin then Cynde. "Better go see what your boyfriend wants."

"He's really only *kinda* my boyfriend."

Mr. Bauer smiled and continued walking.

"Cynde!" Justin called again.

Cynde sighed. "See you tomorrow, Mr. Bauer," she said quietly as she stopped walking.

"See you tomorrow, Cynde." Mr. Bauer called out without looking back.

Justin hurried over and grabbed Cynde's hand.

"C'mon," he said, pulling her down B hall.

He pivoted and continued pulling her down A hall and into D hall, his sandy colored hair flapping. Cynde remembered when she'd found Justin's soft, floppy hair irresistibly sexy along with his bright blue eyes and the light tan patch on his nose. She used to think the patch was a small sunburn from being outside long hours at football practice. But football season was long over, and she now suspected the patch was some sort of birthmark.

"I have to get to French," Cynde finally objected.

Justin stopped and pressed her into the D hall lockers.

"Oui, oui," he said, kissing her.

"Justin…"

"C'mon," he said, again pulling her toward the weight room near the gym. It was locked. "Damn!"

"Justin…"

"Shhh… C'mon," he said, pulling her toward the doors of the gym.

The next classes were still changing in the locker rooms. Only the two gym teachers, Coach Gevin and Mrs. Olsen stood in the gym, chatting. Justin waited for them both to turn away and pulled Cynde into the gym, beneath the bleachers. It was dark and smelled faintly of a combination of popcorn, ammonia, and stale cigarette smoke. Cynde wished she were out smoking with Mr. Bauer, watching him stare up at the sky.

Justin pressed Cynde into the wall and kissed her. After a minute, he lowered his hands from the wall, placing one at the nape of her neck, and the other around her waist.

Mr. Bauer...I might just love you forever.

Cynde kissed Justin back until the bell rang. Then, Justin grabbed her hand again, and they darted out from under the bleachers and through the gym doors.

"See ya at lunch," Justin said, squeezing her hand before turning toward the computer lab.

Cynde made her way to French class.

Two

The ticking of the clock always seemed to grow louder by the very end of the day. Ms. Kaminski was still droning on about the quadratic equation, but Cynde had already begun to pack up. When the bell finally rang, she rushed toward the door.

"I wouldn't be in such a hurry if I were you, Ms. Ehler," said Ms. Kaminski.

"What?" Cynde asked blankly.

"You're a smart girl, Cynde, but you're still not living up to your full potential."

Here we go… Smart girl.

Teachers only wanted to talk about how smart she was when they thought she was stupid.

"High school sets the tone for the rest of your entire life. You want to make wise choices now so that you'll have more choices later."

Cynde had no interest in hearing the rest. She could barely tolerate Ms. Kaminski's nasal voice or stand to look at the way she applied that horrid magenta shade of lipstick straight across her top lip, overlooking the cupid's bow entirely.

Cynde rolled her eyes and continued on her way. She had to hurry if she was going to elude Justin. Jogging past the library, she saw Fat Becky.

"Becky!"

Fat Becky looked astonished to be hearing her name.

9

"Um… Hi, Cynde," she said nervously. Her mouth was colored blue from some kind of candy she was eating.

"Becky. Can you do me a favor?"

"Oh. Um…sure, yeah."

"Cool. I need you to run down to B hall and put my backpack in my locker. It's B36. Here," she continued, tearing a piece of paper from the corner of a notebook then pulling the pencil out of Fat Becky's hand, "I'm gonna write down my combination for you, okay?"

Cynde pulled out her history book and a single notebook, then handed the heavy backpack and the scrap of paper to Fat Becky.

"Thanks, Becky. See ya!" she said, turning to jog down the hall toward the backdoor exit.

"Oh. No problem, Cynde." Fat Becky called out. "See ya tomorrow!"

Cynde exited the school, ran through the back field and up the hill into the lightly wooded area in between the school and the Methodist Church behind it. She hurried through the side of the churchyard and onto West Maple Ave, where she waited. A few minutes later, a shiny white Land Rover Defender pulled up, and Cynde got in. She was able to smell the Armani Acqua di Gio right away.

"Hey, babe," Luke said, looking her over appreciatively. "Lookin' good."

Cynde smiled at him. Luke looked incredible as usual. He had short dark hair, dark eyes, and a perfect smile. He'd once told her that his father was an orthodontist. Cynde thought Luke must've benefited from braces during his teenage years. He reached a tanned, muscular arm around her and gave her a quick squeeze before driving off, turning the volume up on The Fugees' "Fu-Gee-La."

Pulling into the motel parking lot, Luke reminded her to sit and wait until she saw him enter the room. He parked in the back of the lot, grabbed his denim jacket from the backseat, and walked swiftly to the office. A minute later, he was ducking into a room. Cynde let a minute pass, checking her reflection in the rearview mirror and re-applying her cherry lip gloss, then headed in after him.

As soon as she entered the room, Luke took Cynde into his arms and sat on the side of the bed, pulling her down beside him.

"How's my girl, huh?" he asked, kissing her too soon to allow for a response. He pushed her back, then climbed over her. "Aw, fuck, I missed you," he said, burying his face in her neck, kissing her more. "I thought about you all week long. Mmmm… You drive me wild, ya know that?" He continued kissing her, then moved to rest beside her, propping himself on an elbow. "How've you been? How was school?"

"School sucks," she answered.

"Mmmm, you smell good too," he said, kissing her neck, "Fuck, you're so fucking hot."

He slipped a hand up her shirt, cupping and massaging her breast for a moment, then climbed to his knees and pulled her into a sitting position. He raised her arms above her head and lifted her shirt up, casting it aside on the bed, then began fumbling with her bra strap.

He gets it wrong every time.

"It's a front clasp," she said.

11

"Hahaha...shit, I get that wrong every time, huh?" he said, kissing her while removing her bra. He pushed her back onto the pillow, cupping and massaging her breasts one at a time, then ducked down to kiss them.

"How was your trip?" she asked.

"Awful," he said, continuing on her breasts.

"Did you lose?"

"Huh? Oh, no. Vegas was nice," he said, resting on an elbow, reaching his hand over to caress her nipple with his thumb. "I actually won at Blackjack. Saw a couple shows with my buddy. The casino gave us a bunch of vouchers for the buffet. Biggest crab legs I've ever seen. It was a good time. Just, ya know, the whining, the complaining!" He suddenly released a short growl of disgust, startling Cynde. "Nothing is ever good enough!"

Luke rolled onto his back, rubbing his eyes with the palms of his hands. Unsure of what to do, Cynde lightly ran her hand over his chest and down his abdomen, wishing she'd never started him talking. She looked over his body, wondering how long it would be until he removed his clothing. She definitely preferred him naked.

Cynde thought about how he had looked when she'd first seen him in the pool hall. He'd been wearing a white tank top, and she had noticed his body right away. She'd watched him closely, enjoying the stern, focused expression on his face as he bent over the pool table to aim his cue stick, his arm muscles flexing. She had imagined running her hands over his strong arms. His skin had looked so smooth.

She now knew it was actually a bit rough, almost like garnet sandpaper, covered in a fine prickly stubble—remnants of the body hair Luke shaved off every other day. Cynde enjoyed making these little discoveries. She liked knowing the personal details about a man's body.

"You know, I bought her that seven-thousand-dollar tennis bracelet," Luke was saying. "That was my way of buying myself some time, ya know?" She must've looked confused because he clarified, "Ya know... like... instead of a ring."

"Oh," she said.

"Yeah, and like, I don't know... I thought we had an understanding. But apparently, I wasn't clear enough." Cupping his hands around his mouth, he called out, "I'm not fucking ready!"

Cynde listened a few more minutes, trying to appear interested and sympathetic when suddenly, Luke jumped up.

"I almost forgot. I got you something," he said, a smile sweeping across his face. He went over to his jacket on the red upholstered chair in the corner and dug into the jacket's pocket, pulling out a small, green velvet pouch. He handed it to her. "Open it."

Cynde sat up and pulled the drawstring of the velvet pouch. She reached in and pulled out a small crystal bull figurine. She gasped, genuinely astonished by its beauty, and overcome by the thoughtfulness and generosity of the gift.

"Oh, my God, Luke. Thank you!" she whispered, tilting the little bull in her fingers, studying it from different angles. "I love it. Thank you so much."

Luke beamed down at her. "Wow… you really do love bulls, huh?" He reached down and stroked the side of her face. "A girl who appreciates simple things…" he said in awe. "You're a wonder, baby." He took the figurine from her hand, dropping it back into the velvet pouch. "Let's put this away for now."

He placed the velvet pouch aside on a wooden table beside the chair, then stripped down to his black boxer briefs before climbing back onto the bed. Cynde watched each movement of Luke's strong, beautiful body as he pulled off her skirt and her underwear. Resting on an elbow beside her, he raised his hand to his face, stuck his index and middle fingers into his mouth then reached them down between her thighs, inserting the two fingers into her. Cynde inhaled sharply, pressing her lips together to keep from crying out.

Luke had taken her virginity weeks before, but she still found sex quite painful. It did seem to be getting a little easier each time though. Luke stared into Cynde's eyes while moving his fingers inside her.

"Why aren't you ten years older, Cynde?" he asked, removing his fingers. He pulled off his underwear and climbed on top of her. "I'd marry you in a heartbeat."

Three

It was dark by the time Luke dropped Cynde off. Her mother still wasn't home. She could hear the telephone ringing before she'd managed to unlock and open the door. She darted through the dark house to the kitchen and picked up the phone.

"Hello?"

"Holy hell... Cynde! Where on Earth have you been? You disappeared after school. Where were you?"

"Oh... Justin, I'm sorry. I—I wasn't feeling well after school. I actually thought I was gonna puke, so I sat in the girls' bathroom a while, and then I just walked around a little to get some air."

"You walked around until 9'o'clock at night?!"

"Um...no... My mother needed me to go shoe shopping with her," Cynde said, twisting herself in the long telephone cord. "Needed help picking out a pair of kitten heels. Who knew there were so many styles of kitten heels to choose from?" There was silence on Justin's end, so Cynde continued rambling, now twisting the cord around her fingers. "Oxfords, slingbacks, Mary Janes, D'Orsay, ankle straps, t-straps, open-toe, peep-toe—"

"Stop."

"What?"

"Cynde, are you lying to me? I'm not accusing you. It just kinda sounds like you might be lying."

15

"No, Justin. No, I swear. I meant to meet you out front. I just felt sick, I don't know. I'm feeling much better now."

There was a long pause before Justin spoke again. "Alright. Well… I'm glad you're safe. I was pretty worried. Glad you're feeling better too. You'll be at school tomorrow?"

"I'll be there."

"Is your mom home?"

"Nope. Working late as usual."

"Do you want me to come sit with you?"

"No…no, thanks. I have some reading for history, and I'm actually pretty tired."

"Alright. Tomorrow, then, okay? Can I pick you up for school?"

"You know I like to walk in the morning."

"Fine. I'll leave my car home and walk you to school."

"Justin…"

"Yeah, fine. We'll hang out after school then. Okay?"

"Absolutely. Tomorrow. You can come here. My mom will probably be working late again."

"Alright, Cynde. I miss you. I'll see you tomorrow."

"Miss you too. Good night."

"Good night."

Still standing in the dark, Cynde untangled herself from the cord and hung up the phone. She spotted the ten dollar bill her mother had left for pizza. Luke had already fed her, so she pocketed the money then picked up her history book and notebook and brought them to her bedroom.

She turned on her bedside lamp and pulled the small green velvet pouch from her jacket pocket, then walked to her bookcase. On the second to top shelf sat a small hand-carved wooden bull figurine. She dropped the little crystal bull from the velvet pouch into her hand and held it up in the light a moment before setting it beside the wooden bull.

After showering, she dressed in her babydoll pajamas and climbed into bed with her book and notebook. She took notes as she read so that she could review them before class. That way, she'd be prepared in case Mr. Bauer called on her. Then, she set her book on her nightstand, leaving the bedside lamp on.

She lay awake, staring at the walls of her bedroom. They were painted periwinkle, which had been her favorite color at age 11. On the closet door, there was an old poster of The Smashing Pumpkins, her favorite band at age 12. She couldn't remember the last time she'd even listened to The Smashing Pumpkins, but it hadn't occurred to her to take down the poster.

She closed her eyes and thought of Mr. Bauer. Reaching a hand down between her thighs, she thought of Luke's naked body pressed against hers. Cynde hadn't yet figured out how to cum with a man, but she still found sex with Luke exciting. And she'd discovered that, as long as she made the right sounds at the right moments, Luke couldn't detect the difference.

She was still sore but continued touching herself, her thoughts vacillating back and forth between Luke's naked body and Mr. Bauer's strong, rough hands.

'Three hundred ears in 80 minutes," she whispered aloud just before bringing herself to orgasm.

Four

When the lunch bell rang, Cynde walked to her locker to drop off her books. As soon as she opened her locker, she felt Justin's arms around her waist.

"Mannino's?" he asked.

"Nah. Let's just eat in the cafeteria."

"Okay," he agreed, releasing her waist to take her hand.

The line had already stretched to the back of the cafeteria by the time they arrived. Cynde got in line and Justin stood behind her, wrapping his arms around her waist again. They didn't speak other than to respond to the repetitive greetings of peers:

"Hey, Justin! Hey, Cynde!"

"Hey," they'd answer in unison.

Finally, they managed to sit with their trays. Cynde started on her soft pretzel and Arctic Splash iced tea. Justin ate his dreadful looking cheesesteak.

In her boredom, Cynde gazed around the room, her eyes landing on the *Big Picture* bulletin on the wall. Years ago, when she had just started middle school, the district had gotten into a contract with *Big Picture*, a company that had agreed to send out a new giant poster for the cafeteria each semester. It contained one large frame at the top and three smaller frames at the bottom. There'd been a fresh one hung for the start of her 6th grade year and a second one to replace it at the start of the second semester. Then, something had gone wrong. Cynde didn't know what.

Maybe the district canceled its contract. Maybe *Big Picture* had gone under. All Cynde knew was that the second poster from her second semester of 6th grade was the last one that had been hung.

The three smaller pictures contained cutesy illustrations with upbeat aphorisms. The large picture atop was an ad for Burger King. In huge boldface orange font, atop a picture of a Burger King Whopper, it read: *What D'ya Say? What D'ya Say?* Cynde vaguely remembered the old television jingle but it hadn't stuck around long enough for today's 6th graders, or maybe even most other 10th graders to remember it. It hadn't been clever marketing to begin with, but for anyone who didn't recall the jingle, the poster would be completely senseless. Still, no one else ever seemed to notice it.

"Get all your history reading done last night?" Justin asked.

"Yep."

"How're you doing in algebra?"

Cynde only rolled her eyes in response.

"You should let me help you," Justin said, resting his hand over hers.

"I'm getting a C."

"You can do better than that," Justin said. "Let me help you."

Justin was a math genius. He'd started competing in the International Mathematical Olympiad his freshman year. He was now a junior and already trying to decide which ivy league college to attend, with dreams of becoming an actuary or engineer. It wasn't that Cynde didn't admire his skills and ambition, nor that she didn't appreciate his desire to help her; she just couldn't seem to focus on math.

Justin had tried to help her at the start of first semester. Back then, Cynde was still wildly attracted to Justin, just as she'd been the entire previous school year. She'd very much wanted to impress him, but the moment he'd begin trying to explain anything at all, her brain would start to malfunction, and all she could think about was how cute he looked in his letterman jacket, or how adorable his floppy hair was as it fell over his pretty blue eyes, and how intense, focused, and impossibly sexy he looked whenever he talked about math. If his arm had so much as accidentally brushed against hers, it would send shockwaves throughout her body.

Soon after he'd tried and failed to tutor her, Justin had asked Cynde to be his girlfriend, and she'd gladly accepted. It wasn't long before she had started to lose interest though. Now, here they were, 5 months later: Justin and Cynde: Morrisville High School's hottest couple, and she was the only one who seemed to recognize the irony of it.

"This afternoon. Okay?" he asked.

"What?"

"After school. I'll drive you home. Bring your algebra book."

"Right. Sure. Thanks," Cynde said, forcing a smile to keep herself from sighing.

Five

Much to her amazement, Justin's explanations did make sense to Cynde as he helped her through her Algebra II homework. She felt more prepared for the upcoming test Ms. Kaminski had warned the class about too.

"Thanks," Cynde said, smiling across the kitchen table at Justin.

"Anytime," Justin said, taking her hand. "You and math are my two favorite subjects."

Cynde stood up and wandered to the refrigerator.

"Juice?" she offered.

"No, thanks," he replied. "Wanna watch a movie or something?"

"You're inviting me to sit in pink hell?" she asked.

Justin laughed. *Pink hell* was Cynde's name for her living room ever since her mother had snapped a couple years back and painted the entire thing pink, then had matching wall-to-wall pink carpet installed, and hung matching pink sheers and drapes on all the windows. She'd even added a pink sofa and covered it with fluffy pink throw cushions.

"Should we make dinner plans? Can I take you out?" he asked.

"Let's go to your house for dinner."

"Okay. I think my mom is making pot roast."

"Yum!" Cynde said, packing her algebra homework into her backpack.

Cynde liked Justin's parents, and his parents both seemed to like her. Justin's home reminded her of the way her own home used to be... before the advent of pink hell... before she'd started coming home to a dark, empty house... before her father had left.

"Hey," Justin said, grabbing her wrist as she stood up from the table. "I miss you." He rose from the table and wrapped his arms around her waist.

"I'm right here, silly."

He kissed her then cocked his head to the side. "Can I get some alone time with you before we head over to my house?" he asked.

She smiled politely, gesturing toward her bedroom, then lifted her backpack and carried it into her room, dropping it onto her desk.

Justin had followed her. He took off his shoes and sat on her bed, waiting for her to remove her boots and lie back against her pillow. Leaning on his elbow beside her, he reached his arm around her, kissing her. Justin's kisses were soft and sweet, and he always smelled nice, like whatever kind of fabric softener his mother used. Cynde closed her eyes and relaxed, feeling warm and comfortable.

Justin lifted his hand up from the bed and placed it onto Cynde's waist then slowly moved it upward to rest atop her breast just like he always did, kneading it a bit in his palm. His kisses grew more passionate but, after a few minutes, he abruptly pulled away, turning onto his back, just like he always did. He ran his hands over his face and up through his hair. Noisily exhaling, he stared up at the ceiling.

Cynde stared up at the ceiling with him. She didn't know what she was doing wrong. She knew Justin had dated Raina Barbieri last year. Raina was a senior, but Cynde had slept over her house a couple times when she was just 7 years old and Raina was 10. Raina had been a pageant girl. Cynde remembered her entire bedroom being covered in trophies and sparkly tiaras. The following year, Raina's mother had left Raina's father who'd been unable to hold down a job, and had moved Raina in with her rich new boyfriend who was able to afford all of Raina's fancy pageant dresses. But soon after, Raina had dropped out of pageants altogether. She'd become a cheerleader instead and within a few years, she'd practically made her way through the entire football team.

Justin had also dated Julie South who had been a senior last year. Cynde didn't really know Julie, but everyone knew her reputation. Justin certainly wasn't inexperienced. He just didn't seem to want to go all the way with Cynde. Cynde wasn't even really sure why Justin was still dating her at all.

"Is that new? I don't remember that one," he said. He was pointing over at her new crystal bull figurine.

"Oh. Um...no. I've had that a while. It'd just fallen behind the shelf. Found it back there yesterday."

"Ah," he said, taking her hand in his. "Glad you found it."

He leaned over her, kissing her again, then sat up, clearing his throat. "So, you want to head over?"

"Sure," Cynde said, getting up.

Justin took her hand and walked her out to his 1990 blue Ford Taurus. His house was only about ten blocks from hers. It was bright yellow with white trim. The small front yard was neatly landscaped, and every month, his mother would hang a new seasonal flag out front. The current one had tulips on it and said *Think Spring!*

Justin and Cynde entered the house. There was an aquarium full of angelfish just inside the living room. Justin had told Cynde that his mother bought the fish once he'd started driving. He suspected his mother missed feeling needed, but his father wouldn't allow her to bring a puppy into the house, so she settled for fish.

His father was seated at the desk in the living room, filling in numbers on some kind of spreadsheet on their computer. He looked like an older version of Justin—a tall, handsome man with bright blue eyes and a full head of the same sandy colored hair. He reminded Cynde of a model out of an L.L. Bean catalog—the guy who'd attended a fancy prep school before college and now enjoyed a life full of hiking, sailing, and playing tennis.

"Hi, Mr. Helvig."

"Cynde! Good to see you. How's Justin treating you?"

"Great."

"That's what I like to hear," he said smiling. "Justin, your mother's in the kitchen. Why don't you set a place for Cynde at the table, and see if she needs any help?"

"Alright, Dad," Justin replied.

"See you in a few!" Mr. Helvig called after them as they left the living room.

Entering the kitchen, Cynde saw that Mrs. Helvig was at the island, chopping vegetables for a salad. She had the radio tuned to some kind of cooking station. Mrs. Helvig also looked like she'd stepped out of a magazine. She wasn't striking like Cynde's own mother, but pretty in a neat and somewhat old-fashioned sort of way. Cynde had examined Mrs. Helvig's shoulder-length blonde hair on a few occasions, trying to decide if its soft bouncy wave was natural or if a lot of time was spent making it look that way.

"Hi, Mrs. Helvig."

"Cynde! Justin didn't tell us you were coming. Justin, honey, go set a place for Cynde at the table." Justin turned toward their corner cabinet to collect the dinnerware. "It's so nice to see you. How's Justin been treating you?"

"Oh, just fine, Mrs. Helvig. He's been helping me with algebra again."

"Ah! Put that brain of his to good use. Smart girl!"

Smart girl...

"Can we help with anything else, Mom?"

"No, you two go sit down. Dinner will be ready in just a few minutes."

***

The next morning, Cynde was late getting up. She called out for her mother to braid her hair. When there was no response, she realized her mother had not come in the night before.

Working late, my ass...

Cynde showered and pulled her hair into two loose pigtails tied just below her ears and slipped into her mini cream and white gingham dress then threw on her denim jacket and laced up her combat boots. She picked up her backpack and stepped outside. The weather was cool but sunny...perfect. She stepped back into the house, chucked her backpack toward the back of the hallway closet, and pulled out her skateboard.

Cynde's skateboard was her most prized possession. It had plain white griptape and a hot pink deck with a custom gold and white stencil design of a bull. She headed back outside with her board. She didn't have a plan, but anything was better than school.

Six

Cynde usually avoided West Bridge Street whenever she was ditching school. She never knew when she could expect Officer Gallo to pass by in his cruiser. That guy had nothing better to do than stop and hassle her for cutting class or for being out too late. She couldn't count the times he'd stopped and ordered her into his backseat to lecture her about common sense and safety, and drive her home. A few times, he'd even walked her to her front door to lecture her mother.

But today, Cynde was feeling a bit reckless. She skated straight onto West Bridge. She passed Russo's Tavern, Gene's Barbershop, Jule's Tires, and kept right on going. When the sidewalk ended, she tucked her board under her arm and kept walking, aimlessly yet somehow still determined.

Suddenly, a huge semi truck swung out into the middle of the tight intersection before her. She stopped short, terrified, clutching her board in front of her. She was sure the truck was about to wreck.

But it didn't wreck. It kept right on turning, rapidly swinging the long trailer out behind it at what looked like an impossible angle. She squinted against the sun to get a look at the driver but could only make out a bulky shouldered silhouette and a baseball cap. As the truck continued turning, she was able to see through the partially opened window. The driver had a scraggly golden mustache and beard and wore a blank expression. Cynde continued to stare on in amazement as he seemingly effortlessly rounded the trailer through the rest of the tight corner then drove on down the road.

She realized he must be driving to the nearby truck stop. The road looked fairly level and had a nice slight bend; a good road for skating. Hopping back onto her board, she skated down to the truck stop. Once there, she recognized her trucker right away.

He'd parked and was now walking around his truck, inspecting it. The lot seemed otherwise empty, so Cynde picked up her board and scooted behind a trailer to watch him. He was wearing a faded blue t-shirt and jeans. He had love handles and a bit of a jelly belly over a big, strong frame. His arms and legs looked thick and solid. She wondered how old he was. Luke was 28. She thought the trucker might be just a bit older than Luke, but she couldn't be sure.

She studied his wide chest, able to see a bit of hair sticking out at the neckline of his t-shirt. Cynde had never touched a man's chest hair. She tried to imagine what it would feel like beneath her fingers as she thought about him maneuvering through that tight intersection, suddenly feeling an urgent desire to touch this man. It wouldn't have to be anything more than that; she just needed to touch him. But how? How would she even get close to him? What could she say?

Without realizing it, Cynde had inched closer toward the edge of the trailer she was hiding behind. When her skateboard unexpectedly made contact with the trailer, she startled, and the skateboard dropped from her arms, clattering to the ground. The trucker looked up from where he was standing. She stood frozen at the edge of the trailer as he stared directly back at her.

"Hello there!" he called to her.

Cynde took a step to the side, away from her skateboard, unable to speak.

"Hey, darlin," he said. "Are ya lost?"

Cynde remained frozen. She couldn't think of what to say to this stranger who'd just caught her spying. She wanted to grab her skateboard and take off but couldn't seem to get her body to cooperate. The man took a few steps in her direction.

"Do you need help?" he asked, looking concerned.

"No," Cynde finally managed.

"I can use my radio to get you help. Are y'alright?"

"Yes."

"Are ya sure?"

"Yes," she repeated.

"Can I give you a lift somewhere?"

"No. Um...no."

"Okay. You seem a little shaken. I'd like to help if I can. Would ya like some water? I have water in the truck."

Cynde nodded.

"Yeah? Alright. C'mon over. I'll getcha a water," he said, turning back toward his truck.

Cynde followed him. She stood watching as he opened the passenger door, climbed up, and reached in. A moment later, he turned back and jumped down from the truck with a small, unopened bottle of Deer Park, handing it to her.

She stared at his hand holding out the water.

Touch him. Do it. Touch him.

She reached out and took the bottle of water.

Damnit.

She held the bottle, continuing to stare at him.

"Ya wanna sit?" he asked, gesturing toward his truck. "It's pretty comfortable." He held up his hands. "I ain't gonna hurtcha. Promise."

Cynde nodded. He smiled at her.

"Yeah? Alright. C'mon, darlin," he said, holding out his hand to help her climb up.

Cynde looked at his outstretched hand, feeling a surge of excitement. Pressing her lips together, she reached out and took his hand. The physical contact sent a jolt through her entire body. His hand was big and warm and a little bit rough, although softer than she'd expected. She wished she could hold his hand a while longer, but after helping her up into the truck, he pulled it away, slamming the door closed.

Cynde had never been in a semi truck before. The cabin was much roomier than she'd expected. She glanced around, noticing the small shelving unit containing a neatly folded pile of clothing and, behind that, there was actually a bed with a green wool blanket and a pillow. She'd never known there were beds inside semi trucks. It actually looked like a cozy place to sleep.

The driver's side door opened, and her trucker climbed in, removing his baseball cap, setting it on the dashboard. His hair, the same golden color as his scraggly beard, was thick, a bit shaggy, and looked a little greasy.

"I'm Todd," he said.

Todd the trucker.

"What's your name?"

"Cynde."

"Cynde," he repeated. "It's very nice to meet you, Cynde. Are ya feeling okay?"

Cynde nodded.

"Do you live around here?"

She nodded again.

"You do! Good. Would ya like me to getcha home?"

"No. I'm just sort of wandering around today."

"I see. Ya come to this truck stop often?" he asked with a crooked grin.

"No," Cynde replied. "I just decided to come check it out for the first time today."

"Fair enough," he said. "How do you like it so far?"

"I like it," Cynde said, smiling shyly.

"Hey! It's good to see you smile, Cynde," he said, smiling back at her.

He had a dimple in one cheek peaking out from behind his short, scraggly beard. The urge to touch him again had grown so strong, she tucked her hands beneath her thighs to keep herself from doing it. At this point, she realized what a lunatic she must seem like to this man. She'd have to try a bit harder to show him she was a normal person. She wanted him to like her.

"Do you live around here?" Cynde asked.

"Well, I mostly live in this truck, but my home is back in Nebraska," Todd said.

Nebraska!

Registering the excitement in her eyes, he smiled, "You like Nebraska!"

"Oh, yes…" she gushed. "I mean… Well, I've never actually been there, but it seems like a really nice place."

"Huh. Well… yeah… It is a nice place," he agreed. "Lots of farmland. I was actually raised on a small farm, but now, I've got a studio apartment in Omaha. Like I said, I'm not there too much, but it's good to have a place of my own to rest my head when I am."

"Have you husked a lot of corn?" Cynde asked.

Todd laughed. "Sure…sure."

"Are you fast?"

He laughed again. "Well, the combine is pretty fast. That does most of the pickin."

"Oh."

"Well, don't sound too disappointed. They still hold annual competitions at the state fair for speed husking in order to celebrate the tradition. But machines do most of the work now. Most farms switched to machines long before I was born… even before my father was born."

"Oh," Cynde repeated.

"Well, now, there are still a few small farms around that do everything by hand…. old guys still practicing the old ways of their grandpas. They've got their arguments for why the old ways with horses and wagons are superior."

"Really?" Cynde asked, intrigued. "Like what?"

"Well, you can grow feed for horses. You can't grow gasoline. And you can raise your own replacement horses."

"Right," Cynde said, brightly.

"And horses don't cause compaction of the soil."

Cynde smiled. Those seemed like very sound arguments to her.

"Also," he continued, "Farmers probably had a stronger community before machines. Neighbors used to rely on neighbors. Everyone needed extra hands to get the work done back in the old days. Now, people are much more independent... which is good in some ways, I guess, but bad in others. Ya know... people still need people... even if the machine convinces them otherwise."

Cynde peered into Todd's eyes. They were a deep blue. She re-examined the rest of him, her gaze again falling on the little hairs sticking out of the neckline of his t-shirt. She wanted so desperately to touch him. She could feel her heart rate speeding up as she worked up the nerve.

Finally, she took a deep breath and dove over into his lap, mashing her lips against his. She wrapped her arms around his neck and kissed him more fiercely than she'd ever kissed anyone. And, much to her relief, Todd kissed her back.

Seven

Cynde enjoyed the feel of Todd's fuzzy mustache over her lips, the warmth of his hand pressed across her shoulder blades, and the weight of his other arm which he had wrapped gently around her waist as he continued kissing her. Finally, she eased her grip and pulled back to look at him. His deep blue eyes began searching her face right away.

"That was… unexpected," he said.

"Oh," she said, dropping her head. "I'm sorry."

"No," he said, touching her face. "It was nice. It was *very* nice, just… unexpected."

She smiled, snuggling into him a bit.

"So, Cynde…" he said, resting his arms loosely around her, "Tell me what you're doing at this truck stop today."

"Oh, I—I—" she stammered.

"It's okay. I'm not gonna judge. I get the feeling this isn't something you've done before," he paused. "Is it?"

Cynde shook her head.

"So, do you want to tell me what you were thinking, coming here this morning?"

Cynde was silent.

"Again, no judgment from me. You just seem like a sweet girl, and I'd hate to think of you getting yourself into a scary situation."

37

Cynde nuzzled her face into his neck a bit, enjoying his smell. It was sort of warm and salty.

"So, why don't you tell me what's brought you here?"

"You," Cynde answered shyly.

"What?"

"You brought me here."

"How do you mean?"

"Well, I was walking down Bridge Street, and I saw you drive through the intersection, and I just wanted to— Well, I wanted to meet you."

"You wanted to meet me?"

Cynde nodded.

"Me, specifically?"

"I just thought you were... well... kinda cute, I guess," she said, lowering her head to his chest, hiding her face.

"So... you're okay? You didn't come here to—?" he broke off. She slowly raised her eyes to look at him. "...work?" he finally finished.

"Work?" she asked blankly. That's when it hit her. "Oh!" She laughed. "Oh, no... Do you think I'm a hooker, Todd?"

She continued laughing. He chuckled a bit uneasily with her.

"Well, to be clear, I..." he paused. "No, I didn't think you were a hooker. I just thought you were a nice girl who was... maybe thinking she was out of options."

She lifted herself up to look directly into his deep blue eyes.

"You're so nice," she said.

Todd laughed again.

"No, really," she said.

"So…" he paused, "You really just followed me here on a whim?"

"Yeah," she shrugged.

"That's— Well, that's even wilder than what I thought," he marveled. "You crazy girl…" his voice trailing off.

He brought his hand to her face, brushing his thumb over her cheekbone. Cynde leaned in and kissed him again. Todd kissed her back as she lifted his hand to her breast. He cupped it, groaning into her mouth. Cynde felt tingles all over, knowing the sound of Todd's deep groan would live inside her forever.

Abruptly, he pulled back from her. He sucked in a breath of air and blew it out noisily. He smiled, but she thought he suddenly looked uncomfortable. She tried to kiss him again, but he turned his head away.

"Mmmm… Darlin, I'm gonna have you sit over there now, okay?" he said, gesturing toward the passenger seat, his voice sounding tight.

"Oh," Cynde said, getting up from his lap and moving to the passenger seat.

She looked around awkwardly. Todd shifted in his seat, then lifted his head to stare upward at the cabin roof. She stared up with him, confused. What had she done wrong? Why were guys so weird?

"So," she began quietly, "I guess you don't want to—?"

"Oh, yeah, I do," he said. "Trust me, I do. You're a very pretty girl, Cynde... a very *sweet* and very pretty girl. But... well," he swallowed, "Ya seem awful young."

"I'm 17," Cynde lied, immediately wishing she'd said 18. She was pretty sure she could have pulled off 18.

"Hmm," he said followed by a short whistle.

18, you idiot! Always say 18!

"Darlin, you're a pretty little thing, but I've gotta let you go."

Embarrassed, Cynde turned to open her door. Todd caught her wrist.

"Hey," he said. "I wantcha to know something."

Once again, Cynde looked into Todd's deep blue eyes.

"You're the wildest thing that's come into my life in a long time," he said solemnly. "I'm never gonna forget you, Cynde."

Cynde smiled. She leaned in and kissed him once more. He returned her kiss, lingering just a moment before pulling back. She opened the door and climbed down from his truck, walked over to her skateboard, and skated away.

Eight

Cynde returned home well before the time she knew she could expect Justin at her door. She changed into her babydoll pajamas then decided to paint her fingernails and toenails apple green. Once they dried, she climbed into bed, pulling the covers up to her chin, and soon drifted off.

Justin knocked before opening the door.

"Cynde?"

"In here!" she called from her bedroom.

"You're supposed to lock the door!" he called back, walking to her room. "Sick or skipping?" he asked, sitting on her bed.

"A little bit of both?"

"No more skipping, Cynde. You need to keep your attendance up."

"Okay, Dad."

"I stopped by Ms. Kaminski's room. She gave me your math homework."

"Ugh… Ms. Kaminski…"

"She's not so bad. She's just kind of a dull math teacher."

"As opposed to all the really exciting math teachers?"

"Yeah. Like me," he said, leaning over to kiss her.

He tried to sit up again, but Cynde pulled him back to her. He brought his lips back down. After a moment, he climbed over her, lowering his body onto hers.

Figures. I finally get him on top of me, and I'm trapped beneath a fleece blanket and a down comforter.

He continued kissing her, and soon, even through the two blankets, Cynde could tell that Justin was ready to be with her. She reached up and touched his face, making eye contact to let him know she was ready too. But Justin rolled over onto his back, beside her. Cynde looked over at him. His eyes were closed, his lips pressed together. He deeply inhaled, loudly exhaled, then stared at the ceiling.

"I uh… I dropped your homework in the kitchen," he finally said. "Should we do it in there?"

"In the kitchen?"

"Yeah. I'll grab a pencil from your desk."

Algebra. He wants to do algebra.

***

With Justin's help, Cynde finished her math homework, and they ordered a pizza. Justin refused to leave until her mother got home.

"She might not come home. She didn't last night."

"You should have called me, Cyn. I would've come over."

Cynde shrugged. "Makes no difference to me if she's home or not."

"Still. Call me next time, okay?"

"Okay."

Justin took her hand and held it against his cheek, nuzzling his face against it in between kisses. Cynde watched him. There was never a shortage of affection from Justin. It's just that it never went anywhere.

"What's that little patch on your nose from?" she finally thought to ask. "Is it a birthmark?"

"No, it's just a small patch of scar tissue. It's gotten much smaller, but it'll probably always be there," he said. "Why? Is it ugly?"

"No, it's cute," she said, leaning over to kiss the patch. "What's it from?"

"Boxing. Got my nose busted up pretty bad. It healed quickly, but left me with the scar."

"Boxing?!"

"Yeah. I used to box."

"Why did you quit?"

"I quit right after I got my nose busted. Freaked my dad out a little too much. He was worried about concussion. You know… Can't be a math wizard if my brain gets too scrambled."

"True," she agreed. "Still, I wish I could have seen you box."

"My mom recorded every one of my fights. I can go get the videos if you want to see them."

"Oh, my God, go get them!"

"Alright," he said, bending over to kiss her. "I'll be right back."

Justin would only be a few minutes, but soon after he left, Cynde's mother got home.

"Cynde?"

"Hey."

"Sorry, hun. I've gotten all jammed up lately."

"I'll bet."

Her mom stopped and gave her a warning look. Cynde's mother was a beautiful blonde. Cynde had gotten the dark hair from her father. She used to wish she'd been born blonde too, but now she was grateful not to look exactly like her mother. She'd gotten the big crazy eyes and the stupid alien face nose, but at least her father had given her something to remember she was his.

"Excuse me?"

"Nothing."

"You know, I'm working very hard."

"Yeah, it really seems like you have been... working... very... hard."

"If you have something to say to me, you can just say it," her mother said, standing in the kitchen entry way, hands on her hips.

"Well, that's the thing, ma," Cynde said. "I've got nothing to say to you. So, why don't you scamper on back to your boyfriend. Hopefully, this one isn't married."

"You know, Cynde, I understand why you're angry. If I were you, I'd be angry too. But all of this resentment you have toward me is completely misdirected."

"Is it?"

"Your father is the one who ended our marriage!"

It was at least the tenth time Cynde had heard her mother shout this at her. It would usually prompt a rush of sympathy for her mother or at least shame Cynde into silence. But Cynde was no longer feeling so charitable, and she no longer believed all of what her mother told her.

"Bullshit, Donna."

Her mother's mouth fell open. "Your father ended our marriage as soon as he went on that 'business trip,'" she said, holding up air quotes with her fingers.

"Why do you think he went on that 'business trip'?" Cynde asked, mockingly holding up air quotes.

Her mother stood silent.

"Maybe it's because of all the whining and complaining he heard at home. Nothing was ever good enough!" Cynde heard herself shout. "Did you really think your snatch was so precious he was just gonna stick around and get abused for it?!"

"Cynde!" her mother hissed.

"Yeah. *Cynde*. That was your big contribution. Dad reviewed my homework. Dad came to my swim meets. Dad bandaged my knees every time I fell off my skateboard. Dad fixed up that stupid 1968 Citroen you just had to have, even though he was the one who warned you not to buy the piece of shit in the first place. He drove me to my first school dance in that ridiculous car. He sat with us every night for dinner. We were a family! Dad motivated me to do my best. He gave me confidence."

Cynde felt her throat tightening and could hear her voice breaking, but she kept ranting.

"And what did *you* give me? *Cynde.* What a stupid fucking name. It's not even a name. You gave me someone else's nickname. And you couldn't even be bothered to spell it correctly!"

Cynde wasn't sure when Justin had arrived, but when she finally stood up from the table, there he was, standing just a few feet behind her mother.

Cynde gasped and her mother, who now had tears in her eyes, spun around.

"Um... Hi, Mrs. Ehler."

"It's Hardick, Justin. Ms. Hardick."

"Right. Sorry, Ms. Hardick."

"Yeah," Cynde said. "Cause that's a name you'd wanna go rushing back to. Donna wanna hard dick. 'Bout sums it up, I guess."

Her mother stomped toward her. For a moment, Cynde thought she might actually slap her. Maybe she'd kick her out of the house. Cynde half hoped she would. But she only stared at Cynde, her black mascara beginning to creep down her beautiful alien face. Then, she brushed past her and started up the stairs toward her bedroom.

Justin set the two videotapes he'd brought over onto the kitchen table and rushed to put his arms around Cynde. Cynde's body was still buzzing with agitation. She squirmed to escape Justin's embrace, but he only held her tighter. She struggled against him harder, but Justin clamped his arms around her until she was unable to fight anymore.

46

As her body tired, the delicate fragrance of fabric softener and familiarity began to soothe her. She took a deep breath of it and snuggled into Justin's chest. Justin held her another minute then finally released her. He took her hand and walked her to her bedroom. Exhausted, Cynde climbed into bed in the dark room, turning onto her side. Justin climbed in beside her and wrapped his arm around her. It was the first night she slept without her bedside lamp in over two years.

Nine

Justin had a math meet after school, so Cynde walked home alone. The phone started ringing as soon as she got inside.

"Hello?"

"Hey, babe."

"Hi, Luke."

"I wanna see you."

"When?"

"Now."

"Okay. Come get me."

"See ya soon," he said. "Oh, hey! Wear something cute for me, like a gray plaid miniskirt with knee socks, and a little white top."

Cynde glanced down at herself to see the outfit Luke just described then walked over to the front door to look out.

There was Luke, waving from the window of his Land Rover.

"I got a cell phone," he said. "You're the very first person I called."

"I'll be right out," Cynde said, rushing to the kitchen to hang up the phone. She ran to the bathroom, checked her reflection, smoothed on a coat of cherry lip gloss, then ran out and got into to Luke's car.

49

"Hey, cutie!" Luke said. "Damn, you're lookin good."

"Hey," Cynde said. "Where's the cell phone?"

Luke reached into his pocket and pulled out the little black phone. It said *Nokia* just above the screen and had a little antenna.

"Cool!"

"Yeah. Now I can call you whenever I want," he said, reaching an arm around her and giving her a squeeze before driving off.

He turned up the volume, and they listened to Ginuwine's "Pony" while driving to the motel.

Luke pulled Cynde onto the bed as soon as they got through the door. He rolled her onto her back and climbed on top of her.

"Mmmm, I missed you, babe," he said in between kisses. "Goddamn, you're fuckin hot."

He stopped kissing her a moment, looking down into her eyes. She smiled up at him.

"I want you to suck it for me," he said.

"Oh, okay," Cynde replied.

Luke hadn't wanted her to do that since before he'd taken her virginity, but Cynde didn't mind doing it.

He rolled onto his back, and Cynde began to unfasten his pants.

"Wait. Take your clothes off first," he said.

Cynde stood and walked over to the chair where she removed her clothing then returned to the bed and finished opening Luke's fly. He hiked his pants and underwear down, and Cynde pulled them from his legs, dropping them off the side of the bed.

She lowered her head and went to work, listening to Luke moan. She liked the noises he made. Luke pressed down on the back of her head and held it in place.

"Look up, baby. I want to see those eyes."

Cynde raised her eyes up to look at Luke.

"Oh, my God, you're so fucking hot like that," he said. "Keep looking at me, okay?"

He released her head. Cynde held Luke's gaze as she returned to bobbing up and down on him, listening to his heavy breathing. She enjoyed watching his forehead furrow, his eyes twist shut, and his mouth open wide. She liked the way he smelled, mostly like Acqua di Gio and Irish Spring soap but with a faint hint of a warm, salty smell.

The warm saltiness reminded her of Todd. She closed her eyes and thought of Todd, imagining she was listening to his heavy breathing instead. She thought of his scraggly golden beard, his deep blue eyes, the little dimple on his cheek, and the way he'd called her "darlin."

I'll never forget you either, Todd. I'll probably love you forever.

"Hey, I said keep your eyes open," Luke scolded, lifting her up and rolling her onto her back.

"Sorry, Luke."

"It's all good, baby," he said against her lips, kissing her. "Mmmm... Fuck, you're sexy."

He lifted himself off of her.

"Hey, turn around for me...onto your knees, okay?"

Cynde hesitated.

He laughed. "Don't worry, baby. I'm not gonna fuck you in the ass."

Cynde smiled and turned over, climbing onto her knees.

"Damn, girl. You shoulda seen your face," Luke said, still chuckling. "Sorry for the scare," he said, giving her behind a light spank.

***

After leaving the motel, Luke invited Cynde to get sushi. The idea of putting raw fish into her mouth was appalling to her. She didn't want to seem like a child though, so she just said she wasn't hungry.

"Alright. I'll just drive you home. I'll call you tomorrow, okay? The warden's gonna be visiting her bitch mom this weekend, so I'll have some time for you."

Cynde smiled. Luke turned up Busta Rhyme's "Woo Hah!! Got You All in Check" and drove. When he pulled up to her house, she reached over to kiss him goodbye. He pulled her in, kissing her longer than usual.

"Sorry again for spooking you back at the motel," he said, starting to laugh. Cynde laughed with him until he kissed her again. "Miss you already, babe. I'll call you soon."

"Alright. See ya, Luke," she said, climbing out of his Land Rover.

Cynde swung the door closed and turned toward her house. She froze. Sitting on her front steps was Justin. She could tell from his face that he'd seen everything. Luke sped off. Cynde stood listening to the booming bass of his sound system drop in volume, the pitch bending as he drove further away. Finally, she took a step up onto the curb. She took a few more steps toward her house then paused, turned the other direction, and ran down the sidewalk.

Ten

"Cynde!" Justin called. "Cynde, you stop right now!"

She stopped short, standing in place on the sidewalk, wincing as she listened to Justin's approaching footsteps. After a minute, she heard him stop immediately behind her.

"Justin..."

"Don't talk," he said quietly. "Get into the house."

Queasy with panic, Cynde turned and walked back toward the house. Justin walked behind her, waited for her to unlock the door, then followed her inside. Worried that her mother could arrive home any minute, Cynde headed straight back to her bedroom. Justin followed her into her room and closed her bedroom door.

"Sit," he said.

Cynde sat on her bed.

"Justin, I'm so sorry," she said, burying her face in her hands.

"Don't talk. Look at me."

Cynde looked up at him and right away, she could feel her eyes starting to burn. She'd never wanted to hurt Justin.

"I'm going to ask you some questions, and I want you to answer them honestly," he said. His voice was stern, but surprisingly calm.

"Okay."

"How long have you been seeing that guy?"

"Um... I don't know. Not long."

"How long?"

"A month—"

"A month?!"

"No, maybe two months."

Justin's eyes bulged slightly, turning a bit glassy as he shifted his glance away from her. He clicked his tongue.

"What's his name?"

"Luke."

"Luke," he repeated. "Luke," he said again. He took a deep breath. "Luke's got a cool car. I bet he's a really cool guy, huh? Hey, how old is Luke?"

"Justin—"

"N-n-n-n-no. Don't talk, Cynde. Just answer my question. How old is Luke?"

"28."

"28?!" he shouted, suddenly seeming outraged. "My God, he's a fucking pedophile!"

Cynde stood up. "I'm not a child, Justin."

"Oh, is that it?" he asked, his voice lowering. "You're a big girl, Cynde? I'll bet Luke treats you like a big girl, doesn't he? Is that it?"

"Justin, I—"

"You what? What?!"

"I wanted to be with you. I— I don't know why you didn't want to be with me."

"I didn't want to be with you?" he asked, furrowing his brow. "That's what you think?"

Cynde felt hot tears starting down her face. "You were with Raina. You were with Julie. But you've never wanted to be with me."

Justin rubbed his hands over his face. "Oh, my God..." he said. "Oh, my God..."

"It's true."

"It's *not* true," he snapped back. "Those girls wanted to be with me. Ya know why? Because I'm a fucking football player. They were girls who dated me even though I was younger because I seem like a cool guy and I'm good for a good fucking time. That's all those girls want. And that's all there ever was to it with either of them," he said, sitting on her bed.

Cynde sat beside him. Justin dropped his face into his hands, sitting quietly a moment before looking up at her.

"You were different," he said, his voice tightening. "At least, I thought you were. I thought—" he broke off, laughing bitterly as he stood up again. "I thought you were a virgin, and I was afraid to—"

"Justin—" Cynde began, standing and reaching for him.

"No!" he said, pulling back. "You and your mom... You're such sad fucking messes, and I thought you needed someone on your side, someone to look out for you," he said, his voice wobbling a bit. "I thought I was protecting you," he said accusingly.

Cynde sobbed miserably.

"But that's not what you wanted, is it?" he asked, his face twisting in disgust. "No, you wanted a cool guy."

"No," Cynde whispered.

"You wanted a good fucking time."

"No," Cynde repeated.

Suddenly, Justin shoved her backwards onto the bed. He leaned over her, taking hold of her shoulders, pressing her down.

"You wanted someone to push you down and show you what you are."

Do it, Justin. Do it.

He stared down at her, his eyes narrowing. Cynde lay still, staring back at him.

"Fuck you, Cynde," he said, releasing her. He stood up, turned around, opened her bedroom door, and left.

Eleven

Cynde hadn't slept much, but she got up and went to her closet to select an outfit for school. Nothing looked right. She finally chose a pair of baggy overalls and a white t-shirt. She tied her hair into pigtails, grabbed her red hoodie and backpack, and headed out for school.

She managed to get to homeroom on time, and sat in the back as usual. She folded her arms over the desk and rested her head on them.

"Hey, Cynde," a girl's voice called.

"Hey," she said without looking up.

"You and Justin going to Spring Fling?"

"Nope."

"Aw...why not? It's gonna be fun!"

Cynde looked up to see Kathy Jacobs standing over her. Kathy had dyed her hair the same reddish purple color every girl had dyed their hair at least once in the past 5 years. The vibrant shade seemed to highlight the cystic acne covering Kathy's cheeks and forehead. Otherwise, Kathy was a cute and stylish girl, but Cynde found her very dull.

"We broke up," Cynde told her, resting her head back on her arms.

"Oh, no! But you two are so cute together. What happened?"

"I...uh... I don't want to talk about it."

By lunch, everyone seemed to know. Justin was sitting with the football players, and a swarm of girls had come over to sit with Cynde. It didn't seem to matter how many times she said, "I don't want to talk about it." They continued to pry.

Vultures.

She wondered how Justin would answer questions. She cringed, thinking about what he might say of her, what she knew he thought of her. A few times, she allowed herself to gaze over at him. He seemed to be having casual conversations. He looked relaxed. Cynde couldn't even manage to eat her soft pretzel. She felt sick. She got up and decided to wander the halls.

During her math test, she felt worse. She couldn't stop thinking about the pained expression on Justin's face. She thought of his sadness and his rage, his final words to her echoing in her mind again and again.

Fuck you, Cynde.

Still, she completed the test before most of the other students, and was confident she'd done well... thanks to Justin.

Smart girl.

Cynde's eyes filled with tears. She folded her arms over the desk and rested her head, silently crying into them.

Someone tapped her shoulder. She looked up to see Ms. Kaminski and her messy magenta lipstick.

"Cynde," she said softly, squatting down to speak face to face. "Do you need to see the nurse?"

"No."

"No? Are you sure?" she asked, then in just above a whisper, "Is everything okay at home?"

"Uh-huh."

"Okay. Well… I know I'm just the math teacher, but I'll be here after school if you'd like to talk."

"Thanks, Ms. Kaminski. I'll be okay."

"Okay, sweetie. You just keep that in mind. I'm here if you need me."

"Can I have a pass to the lav, Ms. Kaminski?"

"I'll write you one now."

Cynde collected her belongings, and left the classroom with her pass to wander the halls. At final bell, she made her way to her locker, then left the building just in time to watch Justin get into his car and drive away.

She walked home and got into bed. She only wanted to sleep. The phone rang several times, but she didn't answer. No one she wanted to talk to would be calling today. She fell asleep listening to the incessant ringing.

Cynde stayed in bed most of Saturday too. Around 3:00 in the afternoon, she decided she ought to get some fresh air. She showered and dressed in her plaid mini jumper dress and a white t-shirt, dried her hair and tied it in pigtails. Then, she laced up her combat boots, grabbed her skateboard, and went out.

She skated down to West Bridge St. and crossed, then continued down Keystone Avenue, turned left onto McKinley and skated until the road ended. Picking up her board, she continued walking along the muddy trail toward the break in the Delaware canal beneath the highway overpass. She walked around the curve of the canal, under the highway, and continued on toward the old defunct railroad tracks.

It had been a while since she'd walked along the tracks. Officer Gallo was always lecturing her about being back there: *"Nothing good ever happens back there, Cynde. It's no place for young girls."* But something about railroad tracks always gave Cynde a sense of hope.

As soon as she reached the tracks, she saw someone perched on the steel rail a short ways down. She got closer and saw it was Paul Shale.

Ew…

The tracks along the grassy canal path looked inviting, but it wasn't worth dealing with the trashy Manor boy. She turned back, retracing her steps.

"That you, alien face?" Paul called out.

Cynde sighed and turned to face him. Paul sat hunched over, his light blonde hair pulled back into a ponytail.

"Hey! It is you! C'mon back. Take a seat."

"No, thanks," she called back.

"Hey, c'mon! Don't make me chase ya! C'mon back."

Hesitantly, Cynde made her way over to Paul.

"Hey, Paul."

"Sit down."

She set her skateboard down and sat on the steel rail across from him. He was drinking from a bottle of malt liquor.

"May I buy the lady a drink?" he asked.

"No, thanks."

"C'mon. Take a drink, ya priss," he said, leaning over, handing her the bottle.

Cynde took the bottle from him, noticing the way his sharp eyes glittered in the sun. They were a pretty crystal blue, but Cynde had always found them a bit unsettling. She found Paul and his demeanor—a strange combination of indifference and hostile resentment—unsettling altogether. She took a gulp, then another, then a third before handing the bottle back to him.

"Heard about the big breakup," he said.

"Yeah," was all Cynde managed to get out.

Fearing she might start crying, she stood up to leave. Paul rushed to his feet, and put an arm around her.

"Hey," he said, "I don't mean nothin' by it. Breakups suck. I know that. Sit down. C'mon. Sit back down," he said, pulling her back down to sit beside him on the rail. "Forget about him. He's probably a faggot anyway."

Cynde tried to stand again, but Paul grabbed hold of her arm. Cynde sighed.

"I'll hang out here a few more minutes," she said, "but not to listen to your trash talk."

"Alright, alright... Just tryna be supportive." He patted her on the back a few times. "So, what happened?"

"I don't want to talk about it," she repeated for what felt like the tenth time.

"Sure ya do," he said. "Girls love to talk about it. Y'always feel better once you've talked about it."

Cynde covered her face in her hands.

"Let it out, alien girl," Paul said, patting her again.

"I just screwed it all up," Cynde said into her hands. "I wasn't seeing things straight, and I ruined everything."

Paul handed her the bottle. She took another gulp and then another before handing it back.

"How'd you manage to do that?" he asked.

"I cheated on him!" Cynde shouted into her hands. It was the first time she'd said it aloud.

"Wow!" said Paul. "This is getting interesting now. Tell me all about it."

Cynde pulled her hands away from her face. "No, I'da'wanna talk about it," she slurred, feeling the warmth of the malt liquor enveloping her. "But thanks, Paul. I do feel a lil better now."

She turned to look at him, noticing he was actually an alright looking guy. He wasn't as tall or as toned as Justin, but he had a strong enough build and a decent enough face. His teeth were a bit jagged though, and his clothes were old and shabby. She looked down at his tattered Dickies and his worn, faded Iron Maiden t-shirt, noticing the small hole in the shoulder. Then something just below it caught her eye.

"Hey! Do you have a tattoo?" she asked.

"Aw, yeah. My cousin did it," he said, pulling up his sleeve.

She gaped in awe. It was a clumsy stick-and-poke tattoo, but still perfectly readable.

"Oh, my God!" Cynde exclaimed. "It's a bull!"

She traced the bull head with the tip of her finger.

"Yeah," Paul said with a small laugh.

"That's me," Cynde said. "I'm the Bull."

"What?"

"Yeah. That's what my dad called me: 'the Bull'."

"That's a strange thing to call a girl," Paul said.

"Yeah," Cynde agreed with a drunken giggle.

"So, why'd he call you that?"

Cynde took a deep breath. "I was on swim team," she began. "Even with my face in the water, I could always hear my dad shouting all the way from the bleachers: 'Pull, Cynde! Pull!' and I always wanted to win for him, so I'd swim faster and faster." Cynde paused to pantomime swimming freestyle with her arms. "Strong... like a bull." Cynde grabbed the bottle from Paul's hand and took a swig. "An' I always won."

She handed the bottle back to Paul and stood.

"Whoa," he said. "Where ya goin?"

"For a walk."

"Alright. I'll go with ya. There's a real pretty spot over there," he said, motioning with his head. "Nice place to sit."

"No, I don't wanna sit. I wanna walk."

"C'mon, it's a walk down the footpath," he said, pointing.

"That goes to the Manor," she said, instantly regretting the strong note of disdain in her voice.

"Yeah, it does," he said, sounding irritated. "But don't worry. I'm not takin' you into the Manor."

He put his arm around her, guiding her onto the footpath. She tried to slink out of his arm, but he moved behind her, taking hold of her shoulders, maneuvering her in between the hill covered in thick brush and a tall chain link fence. She tried shrugging him off her shoulders, but he held tighter. Starting to panic, she tried to twist away. Paul pushed her face first into the chain link fence, pressing his body against her back.

"Just a short ways now," he said into her ear. "You're gonna like it. I promise."

He wrapped his hands around her upper arms and returned to steering her down the footpath. Cynde desperately looked ahead. She knew if she could just get loose, she could run the rest of the way to S. Pennsylvania Ave. She walked a bit further peacefully, then twisted against him once more, trying to free herself.

"What's your rush, girl? We're here," Paul said, pushing her to the ground.

Cynde landed face down in the small grassy clearing. Paul dropped onto her back, pressing her down tightly. She could feel him fumbling with his pants. Soon, he was pulling down her underwear.

"No! Paul, please…" she begged. "Please don't do this, Paul."

"Shhhh," he said into her ear. "Don't worry, princess. I'm not gonna fuck you in the ass."

He finished slipping her underwear down over her boots, then flipped her onto her back.

"Paul, please don't," she cried.

"That's better," he said. "I wanna look at your pretty alien face while I'm screwin' ya."

"No!" Cynde screamed. "Help!"

Paul covered her mouth with his hand.

"Hold still. I'm gonna fuck you way better than that faggot jock ever could. But shit, you probably know that. That's why you strayed."

Cynde whimpered into Paul's hand as he began prodding forward. She started to flail, and he grabbed hold of her wrist, pressing it tightly to the ground. After another push, he had fully penetrated her. Cynde screeched against his hand, tears streaming from the outer corners of her eyes. Paul stared down, grunting and panting over her.

Soon, the fight drained out of her body, and Cynde simply stared back blindly. Paul removed his hand from her mouth and began kissing and biting her lips then licking her face.

"Mmmm...you sure are pretty," Paul said with a groan. "Weird as fuck lookin', but pretty."

Cynde shifted her eyes off to the side, staring up at the sky. Paul kept going, ramming into her again and again, continuing to lap at her face. Eventually, she closed her eyes, listening to his panting and grunting. Something started to stir in her—a tight feeling, a tension. She wondered if she was going to vomit. Then her hands began to tingle and shake.

Oh, my God… He's going to make me cum.

Cynde's vision blurred and her hips started to quiver. She gasped and groaned softly.

"There ya go," Paul said, "Mmmm…" He kissed her, sucking on her bottom lip. "I told ya you'd like it."

Cynde was sickened at the betrayal of her own body. In that moment, she hated herself worse than she hated the trashy Manor boy raping her. Paul pounded her harder, and she began to detect a slight wheeze in his breathing. As he gained momentum, the wheezing got heavier.

That's why he hates jocks. He's an asthmatic. He'll have to quit before he has a full-blown attack.

Just then, Paul climbed to his knees, grabbing hold of her hips. He thrust into her a few more times, grunting loudly, finishing inside her.

Fuck you, Cynde.

He collapsed over her, kissing her one last time, then withdrew and stood up. Gasping for air, he reached to the ground for his pants. He fumbled in the pocket and pulled out an inhaler, confirming Cynde's suspicions. She nearly laughed out loud, watching him puff on it. Then, he pulled his pants on and picked something else up off the ground. It was Cynde's underwear. He made a show of sniffing them before shoving them into his pocket along with his inhaler.

"See, girl?" he said, looking down at her. "You ain't no bull."

Twelve

Cynde lay still in the grass. She'd somehow lost track of time and suddenly became aware it was dark outside. She picked herself up off the ground and began walking back down the footpath, then under the highway, around the curve of the canal, and onto the muddy trail back out toward McKinley Ave.

She stepped out onto the paved street just as Officer Gallo was crawling around the corner in his cruiser. He slowed at the end of McKinley, shining a bright light on her.

"Cynde? Come on over here, hun."

Cynde approached his vehicle as he got out and walked around to the back passenger door. Officer Gallo was a stocky, middle-aged man with thick, wiery dark hair and ruddy cheeks.

"You know the drill," he said. "Get in."

Cynde got into the backseat. Officer Gallo closed the door then walked around to the driver's seat.

"I don't know what it is about you young girls wanting to hang out by those tracks. One of these times, I won't be out here patrolling, and you'll find yourself in a heap of trouble. It only takes once, Cynde," he said. "I know you think I'm hassling you, hun, but I really do care. I'm just trying to keep you safe."

Cynde stared out the window.

"Is your mom home?" he asked.

"I don't know."

"That's the problem. You don't know where she is. She certainly doesn't know where you are," he said. "I'm not trying to give you a hard time, hun. I know things aren't easy for you at home, but you're a smart girl, Cynde. You should know better than to be hanging around those tracks...especially after dark."

You're a smart girl, Cynde. Smart. Girl.

Officer Gallo continued lecturing the rest of the way to Cynde's house. When he saw that Cynde's mother was not at home, he let Cynde out of his car, waited until she got inside, then drove away.

Cynde showered. Then she took a bath and showered off again. She got into her babydoll pajamas and climbed into bed. She stared at the walls, then closed her eyes. Then she opened them again, looking over at her clock radio. It was nearly 11 PM. Unless he'd gone out, Justin would likely still be up reading at his desk.

She thought of his room. It was always neat and fairly plain with cream colored walls and gray carpeting. He had a queen size bed they'd cuddled in many times, and a desk which had displayed a small framed photograph of her. Surely, he'd gotten rid of it. She imagined him smashing the frame and tearing up the picture. Or maybe he'd simply chucked the whole thing into the trash.

Justin...

She needed to see him. She knew he wouldn't want to speak to her, but she needed to see him. If she could just look at him for a moment, she knew she'd feel better.

Cynde got out of bed and pulled a pair of white sweatpants over her pajamas, then threw on her black hoodie and a pair of bobos. That's when she realized it. She'd left her skateboard back at the tracks. She knew she couldn't go back to retrieve it. It was gone.

Cynde felt her lower lip tremble a bit, but gave her head a quick shake. She'd have to mourn the loss of her beloved board another time. Right now, she needed to see Justin. She rushed out the door. It was raining. She pulled her hood over her head and hurried on her way.

It was maybe a 15-minute walk to Justin's house. She smiled at the sight of his car parked out front. Quietly, she approached his house, noticing the new seasonal flag. It had a picture of an umbrella with a few raindrops and said: *April Showers bring May Flowers.*

She crept around to the backside of his house and could hear Ween's "What Deaner Was Talkin' About" playing softly from inside his room. Cynde moved closer to the window, peeking in. And there he was—not reading at his desk but lying atop his bed, dressed in gray and white plaid lounge pants and a white t-shirt, jotting something into a notebook.

Justin…

Cynde continued to watch him another minute, wishing she could curl up beside him. She looked over at his desk. Her picture was still there! Tears stung her eyes. Maybe he didn't completely hate her. Or maybe he just forgot the picture was even there. Maybe she'd already become so meaningless, he hadn't even thought to throw her away; invisible like The Smashing Pumpkins. Staring at the photograph of herself, she felt like a ghost, peering in on someone from her former life.

Maybe I am a ghost...the ghost of a once-smart girl with a stupid fucking name...a doomed fate from the beginning.

She looked back to the bed to find Justin staring right back at her. With a gasp, she leaped back from his window, turned around, and ran back around the side of the house.

She was rushing from his side yard when he caught her in his arm.

"What are you doing here?" he asked.

"Justin, I—I'm—"

"Never mind. It's raining. Get inside."

He took her arm and hurried her into the house, then back to his bedroom.

"Wait here," he said, leaving the room. He returned with a couple towels, drying his own hair. He handed her the other towel.

"You're completely soaked," he said. "Take off the wet hoodie. I'll get you one of my flannels."

Cynde removed the soaking wet hoodie, then the soaking wet bobos, and the soaking wet sweatpants, and stood waiting in her babydoll pajamas. Justin returned from his closet holding Cynde's favorite of his soft flannel shirts. He quickly averted his eyes, chucking the blue and white flannel at her.

"So, what do you want, Cynde?"

"I'm sorry," she responded in a small voice, sliding her arms into the flannel. "I just wanted to see you. I didn't mean to disturb you."

He stood silent, examining Cynde's face for what felt like a long time. She began to tremble, unsure of what he'd say next.

He lifted the covers of his bed.

"Get in," he said.

Cynde froze at the unexpected invitation.

"Get in," he repeated more firmly.

Cynde got into Justin's bed. Justin got in behind her, turning her away from him so that she faced the wall. He reached back to turn off his bedside lamp then wrapped his arm around her. Cynde tried to turn and face him, but he held her in place.

"Just sleep, Cynde."

Cynde closed her eyes, feeling warm and safe, breathing in the delicate fragrance of fabric softener.

"Justin, I—"

"Shhhh," he said. "You look exhausted, Cynde. Sleep."

Cynde slept.

Thirteen

Cynde woke, smelling Justin, and remembered she was in his bed. Once she opened her eyes, she realized she was alone in his room. She got up and checked her clothing still hanging over the back of his chair. They were still wet. She stood in Justin's blue and white plaid flannel, looking around, then decided she'd better put on her wet sweatpants, and picked them up off the chair.

The door opened. Justin stood in his doorway, wearing the same lounge pants and t-shirt he'd worn to bed.

"Don't put those on," he said. "They're wet. Come have some breakfast. I'll put your clothes in the dryer."

"What about your parents?"

"They're out of town this weekend, visiting my Aunt Miriam."

"Oh."

"Breakfast? I made you an omelet."

"Sure. Thanks."

Cynde followed Justin. He stopped in the laundry room to start Cynde's clothes in the dryer, then walked on to the kitchen. They sat across from each other at the breakfast nook. It was a small pine table with a red and white checkered runner down the center. A tall vase of fresh blue and white asters stood at the center, blocking Cynde's view of Justin. Cynde was comforted by the flowers. While grateful to Justin for letting her sleep in his bed, she wasn't so sure she was ready to sit face to face and talk to him.

Justin moved the vase to the side, prompting Cynde to wince. But Justin simply started eating his plain hamburger patty, which is what Justin ate every morning for breakfast. Cynde began eating her omelet. She drank the apple juice he'd set out for her.

"You were talking in your sleep quite a bit last night," he said.

"What—um... What was I saying?" Cynde asked nervously.

"My name was the only word I could make out."

"Oh," she responded shyly.

"So, Cynde, I'm not sure what you're thinking, but I'm gonna go ahead and tell you what I'm thinking, okay?"

"Okay."

"The lack of communication between us has been... destructive," he said. "I wasn't clear in my intentions, and you weren't open about your expectations, your... needs."

Cynde blushed, looking down at her lap. "Justin, I'm—"

"No, I'm going to finish, and then it will be your turn," Justin said, wiping a napkin over his mouth. He took a deep breath, looking across the table at her. "I've been thinking about us a lot, Cynde. I know I missed a bunch of cues. But instead of talking to me and filling me in, you chose to betray me. Would you agree that's accurate?"

"Yes," Cynde replied quietly.

Justin stared expectantly, but she said nothing more.

"Kind of tragic," he finally said. "I always got the feeling that I wasn't able to fully reach you. I just didn't understand why. And now that I do, I don't know how to fix it."

Fuck me, Justin.

"If I'd recognized the problem, or if it had been brought to my attention earlier, I could have rectified it," he said. Leaning forward, his eyes filled with a heated intensity she had only witnessed once before when he'd pushed her onto her bed and held her down. "I *would* have rectified it."

Oh, God, please fuck me, Justin.

"But now..," he continued, sitting back in his chair, "Well, we can try to improve communication. That's what I'm hoping to accomplish here. But now..." he repeated, "there's been this betrayal."

Damnit, Justin, I need you to fuck me.

"So, what are your thoughts, Cynde?"

She stared in silence.

"I'd like to hear your perspective."

Cynde stood up from the breakfast nook. She knew he wanted her to explain herself, but she didn't know how. Instead, she turned and left the kitchen, walking back to Justin's room. In his room, she removed his flannel shirt, then her pajamas, and stood waiting.

"Cynde," Justin soon called out, walking to his room. "I'm trying to— Oh."

He stood in his doorway, gaping. Cynde stood at the center of his room, naked and trembling, full of anticipation and also terrified of rejection.

Justin took a step forward and closed the bedroom door behind him. He continued to stare another moment.

"You know you can't undo what's been done," he said.

She nodded, tears stinging her eyes.

"Get on the bed," he finally breathed out.

She slipped onto the bed. Justin approached, staring down at her while removing his clothing, causing her breathing to turn erratic. Justin was long and lean, but strong and athletic. He no longer looked like her comfortably familiar boyfriend. He was a man, his body a stranger to hers.

Justin climbed over her. Cynde lunged at him, pushing him onto his back, kissing him frantically. Justin returned her kiss, pulling her onto him, holding her naked body tightly against his. He flipped her onto her back. Taking her face into his hands, he looked into her eyes.

"This is what you want, Cynde?"

She nodded.

Justin reached a hand down to guide himself and began slowly pushing into her. As he entered her completely, Cynde sharply exhaled, feeling an overwhelming sense of relief and gratitude. Her eyes welled up and spilled over. Justin wiped away her tears.

"Are you okay?" he asked.

Cynde nodded. "Yes," she whispered.

He began moving inside her. With each gentle thrust into her, he groaned softly against her lips. Cynde stared up at him.

Justin… my Justin… I will love you forever.

She closed her eyes, burying her face in his neck, breathing him in deeply. She ran her hands over his strong back, pressing him further into her, wishing he would remain inside her, covering her body forever. It was the most complete she'd ever felt. It was the freest she'd ever been.

Clinging to Justin, Cynde moaned with pleasure, an intensity building inside her. As her hands began to shake and her eyes rolled back, she clamped her arms down tightly against him. The blood rushed to her face as her body went rigid. She gasped then cried out, her hips and legs convulsing.

Finally, regaining some composure, she looked back up to find Justin staring down at her, a look of wonder on his face. He lowered his lips to hers and continued thrusting until his own body shuddered with release. Once more, he groaned softly, then rolled away, onto his back. After a minute, Justin pulled Cynde to rest against his chest. Together, they fell asleep.

Fourteen

Monday morning was never something Cynde looked forward to, but this Monday morning, she was filled with excitement. Justin was driving her to school today. She'd always insisted on walking before. It was something they'd once fought about. *"I just want to drive my own girl to school,"* she remembered him saying. She'd said something back about *"the importance of maintaining independent lives"* and *"time to think outside of each other."* She rolled her eyes remembering the dispute.

I was so stupid, my Justin.

Cynde dressed in her black, sleeveless mini dress atop a white t-shirt and was about to tie her hair into pigtails when her mother entered her bedroom.

"French braids?" she asked.

"Yes, please," Cynde responded, sitting on her bed.

Her mother went to work French braiding Cynde's hair. They heard a knock, followed by Justin's voice.

"Cynde?"

"Be right out!" she called.

Her mother followed her out to the living room once she finished braiding. Justin was wearing a gray t-shirt over a long-sleeved white shirt and jeans.

He's so beautiful.

"You look beautiful, Cynde." Justin said.

"You're a beautiful couple," her mother said.

Sometimes, Monday mornings are beautiful.

They got into Justin's car. As soon as he turned on the engine, Primus' "Mr, Krinkle" started blasting through the speakers. He quickly turned it off.

"Sorry," he said, starting to drive.

He took her hand and they drove to school in comfortable silence. He parked out front and turned to her. She reached her arms around his neck, kissing him.

"Whoa...what happened to the rule?" he asked.

She giggled, thinking about her *No Kissing in Public* rule.

"Aw, who cares?" she said with a smile. "You never followed it anyway."

"That's because all day long, I dream of kissing you," he said.

"Just kissing me?" she asked.

"Don't start trouble," he said, kissing her cheek. "Come on. School."

They got out of the car. Justin walked around to Cynde and put his arm around her. She wrapped an arm around his waist, snuggling into him, and they walked up to the first set of stairs.

"Hey, Justin! Hey, Cynde!"

"Hey," they responded in unison.

"Looks like the lovebirds are back together!" Kathy Jacobs announced. "So, are you guys going to Spring Fling?"

Justin pulled Cynde in close. "Can I take you to Spring Fling?"

"You can *take me* anywhere at all," she said quietly.

The bell rang and students began filing up the stairs and into the building.

"See ya," Justin said once they entered the building, bending to kiss her. "I like kissing you in public," he whispered in her ear.

Cynde smiled shyly. "See ya."

She turned to head to her locker just in time to catch Paul Shale watching her. He turned and left A hall, heading down B. Cynde began her walk to homeroom, wishing Justin were still at her side.

In first period, she had trouble paying attention to Mr. Bauer as he lectured on and on; something about the Cold War, Cynde thought. Her mind kept drifting, and she wondered if Justin would be coming to visit her before French.

Fifteen

After school, Justin had baseball practice, but he'd driven Cynde home first, promising to come help her with math after he showered. Once home, Cynde got out her history book and tried to read the chapter but found herself reading the same paragraph again and again. She got up to pour herself a glass of juice when the phone rang.

"Hello?"

"Holy shit!" Luke's voice shouted into her ear. "I've called you like a million times. I thought you were dead or something. Where've you been?"

"Oh. Sorry, Luke. I've just been kinda tired lately."

"Well, I'm coming to get you, so limber up, girlie."

"Oh, no!" Cynde gasped. "No. Sorry, Luke. I can't go anywhere."

"Why not?"

"Luke…" she paused, nervously biting her lip, "I'm sorry. I have a boyfriend."

"What?!"

"Um… yeah. I'm really sorry."

"C'mon. What, some high school boy?"

"Well, yeah, Luke. I'm in high school."

"C'mon," he repeated. "He can't give you what I can."

"I'm really sorry," Cynde said again. "But… well, maybe now you can work things out with your girlfriend."

"I'll leave her," he spat. "Is that what this is about? I'll fucking drop her. Done. Baby, you're the one I care about. You're the only thing in my life I look forward to."

"I'm really sorry, Luke," Cynde repeated. "I think I just need to be with someone closer to my age."

"But I was your first," he said. "It was special. And I've always been a gentleman. Never gone buck wild on you once…even though I think about it all the time. I'm always sweet and gentle with you, baby."

"Oh. Um. Thank you, Luke. It's just that I—"

"C'mon. Let me come get you."

"No."

"Cynde, I need you. Just one last time, okay? Let me come get you one last time. Just one last time."

"I have to go, Luke," Cynde said, hanging up the phone.

The phone began ringing again almost immediately. Feeling a bit anxious, Cynde locked the doors and sat on the floor by the front window, hidden behind the pink sheers. Luke soon pulled up in his Land Rover. She could see him in the driver's seat, parked across the street with his cell phone to his ear, ringing her phone again and again.

She wasn't sure what to do, but she was fairly confident Luke would not come up to the door. He'd always been pretty cautious about not being seen outside Cynde's home or school. Mostly, she feared he would still be sitting outside when Justin came to see her after practice. She looked at the clock and realized she had plenty of time. She curled up on the pink carpet and waited, eventually drifting off to sleep, listening to the phone ring.

She woke to banging on the door.

Oh, no!

She sat up and looked out in a panic but Luke's Land Rover was no longer out there. Instead, Justin's car was parked out front.

"Cynde?" she heard Justin's voice calling from outside the front door.

Justin!

She ran to the door, unlocked and opened it.

"Hey," he said, stepping inside the door. "I was knocking for a while."

"Sorry, I guess I fell asleep."

"Where, on the floor? You have weird marks all over your cheek."

"Oh, um… yeah. Kinda cozy actually."

He smiled at her, touching her cheek, then bent to kiss her.

"You left the juice out," he said, looking past her into the kitchen.

"Oh, right," she said, walking to the counter to pour herself a glass of room temperature apple juice. "Want some?"

"No, thanks," he said, sitting at the table. "Ready for algebra?"

"Algebra…" she whined.

"Sit down," he said. "We'll knock it out and have the rest of the night free."

Cynde moved behind Justin and stretched her arms around his shoulders. She ducked down to speak into his ear. "What'll we do with all that free time?"

"We'll decide on that when the time comes. Right now," he said, tapping her backpack, "...algebra."

Cynde scrunched up her face but sat at the table to do her math homework with Justin. She found herself doing a lot of smiling and nodding as he offered what might have been helpful tips. All she could really think about was the way Justin looked when he was on top of her, and how she felt pressed beneath him.

Focus. Get this done correctly, and he'll soon be yours.

Justin stood from the table and began pacing around the room while she worked on her algebra homework. Every once in a while, he'd come close in order to look over her shoulder, causing her scalp and the back of her neck to tingle. Each time, she'd have to stop, take deep breaths, and refocus.

When her homework was finally complete, Justin came over to stand behind her, leaning over her, reviewing her work. She could feel his breath on the top of her head and was very aware of his hand as it moved over the page and his body as it occasionally brushed against her back.

"Uh-oh," he said quietly. "Looks like you missed a minus sign here."

As he pointed out the problem, his body moved closer against hers, his hand inadvertently brushing her wrist. His voice was so soft while his eyes so laser focused on the page. Cynde pressed her lips together and squeezed her hands into tight little balls in order to continue behaving herself. Justin seemed to notice the physical signs of stress, and he put his hands on her shoulders, causing goosebumps to raise on her arms.

"Hey, you're doing really well, Cynde," he said. "This is excellent work overall. You should be proud of yourself."

Correct the math problem. You can have him undressed within the next 3 minutes.

Justin tilted his head to look at her. "Are you okay?"

"Mm-hm." she managed with a smile.

"Okay," he said softly, smiling back. "Just fix this and then, you're all done."

With the last problem corrected, Justin pulled Cynde to her feet and wrapped his arms around her waist.

"Your turn," Justin said quietly next to her ear. "Tell me what I can I do for you, Cynde."

Cynde pressed against Justin and was just about to direct him to her bedroom when she spotted the two videotapes he'd brought over last Wednesday. Wednesday was less than a week ago but somehow, it felt like a very long time had passed. She couldn't believe she'd forgotten about the tapes and knew she had to see them right away.

"Your boxing videos!"

"Uh…"

"Oh, my God, we *have* to watch them!"

"Okay," Justin said with a laugh. "Do we have to watch them *now*?"

"Yes," Cynde said. She removed her boots then carried the videotapes into pink hell.

She put the first tape into the VCR and turned on the television.

"You're sure we need to watch this right now?" Justin asked, removing his sneakers and following Cynde.

"Just one fight, okay?"

"Okay," he agreed. "One fight."

They sat together on the pink sofa, setting several fluffy pink throw cushions on the floor. Cynde clicked the PLAY button on the remote. The video soon came on. It was a bit grainy.

"Where is this?" she asked.

"Philly. Nearly all of my fights were in Philly. This one was at a gym in Fishtown. I trained here in Morrisville though, right over on Osbourne. The guy trains out of his basement. My parents never liked that, but he's a legit fighter and trainer, unlike the sissy stuff you'll find at most of the newer martial arts centers."

Cynde stared at the screen as a younger Justin in black shorts and boxing gloves climbed into the ring with another boy. She noticed right away that Justin's arms and chest, although nicely toned, were considerably smaller back then. He'd also been at least a couple inches shorter. She wished she could make out more of his face, but the head gear he wore covered a lot of it.

The ring was set inside a dingy looking gym. Cynde tried to imagine Mr. and Mrs. Helvig sitting in the bleachers at such a place. Just then, she heard Mrs. Helvig's voice shout "Go, Justin! Wooo!"

The two boys began to swing and almost instantly, Justin knocked the other boy down. Again, Mrs. Helvig could be heard cheering. As the boys began again, Cynde marveled at Justin's fighting posture, his swift movements, and brazen strikes. She lifted the remote and hit the pause button then reached into Justin's lap and began stroking him. He turned rock hard instantly.

"Justin the fighter," she said to herself in a whisper.

"I'd rather be Justin the lover," he said, turning toward her.

She climbed onto his lap, and began opening his pants.

"What if your mom comes home?"

"Nah," Cynde said, dropping to her knees. "If she's not home by now, she won't be back until late."

She tugged at his pants. Justin pulled them down for her, and she removed them completely along with his boxers, setting them aside on the couch. She wrapped her arms around Justin's hips and yanked them forward to the very edge of the couch cushion, then reached up and pushed his shoulders way back. She brought her hand down, taking hold of him, then lowered her mouth onto him, staring upward to watch his face.

Justin looked down in awe as she bobbed her head up and down, holding his gaze, cupping him below in one hand. Justin's breathing grew louder. He kept his hand gently resting on the nape of Cynde's neck, intermittently squeezing it a little. A few times, his mouth opened wide, his eyes closing and his head tilting back for just a moment. Then, he'd quickly lower his face again to continue watching her.

Justin… my Justin… I will love you forever.

Cynde closed her eyes and lowered herself a bit more, wanting to feel him deeper, deeper. She gagged a little, but took a deep breath then continued pressing more and more firmly against her soft palate, pushing down past it until she could no longer pull in air. There, she continued bobbing in slight, jerky motions so as to keep him buried deep in her throat where she wanted him to stay.

Justin's breathing turned rough and ragged. Cynde felt him gripping her neck tightly, his body quivering.

> *My country, tis of thee*
> *Sweet land of liberty,*
> *Of thee I sing*

She pulled up slightly to taste his release, swallowing, then slowly easing away. She rested her face against his thigh, listening to his breathing soften and become even again, feeling the trembling in his legs begin to slow as his muscles began to relax. She heard him take a deep breath and loudly exhale. He placed his hand softly at the nape of her neck.

"Wow...Cynde," Justin said in just above a whisper. "That was... wow."

Cynde lifted her face and smiled up at him, noticing his face was still flushed. She stood up.

"Can I get you some juice?" she asked.

"I'll uh... I'll just have some water," Justin said.

"Okay. Go lie down in my bed. I'll bring it to you."

"Okay."

After filling a glass with water and a few cubes of ice, she carried it into her dark bedroom and handed it to Justin who was tucked in her bed. He took a sip, then another and handed it back.

Cynde took a sip then placed the glass atop her clock radio and slipped into bed beside him. He pulled her head to his chest, and she nuzzled her face into him.

"Oh, my God, Cynde. I'm feeling so good right now. That was like some kind of sorcery," Justin said. "I just need a little time to recuperate."

"Just sleep now, Justin. Hold me, and let's sleep."

***

Sometime during the night, Cynde felt a hand on her ass. Soon, she was being pushed onto her back and could feel someone climbing over her.

No! No! Please, no!

She woke to the sound of her own voice screeching.

"Okay," Justin said, pulling back from her in alarm. "Sorry, I just wanted to—"

"Justin!" she said, coming to her senses. She reached up and pulled him back onto her, breathing a heavy sigh of relief. She ran her hands down his back, pressing him into her, kissing him.

"Wait," Justin said, pulling back from her. "Jesus, Cynde, that was really scary."

"Sorry."

"What was that about?"

"I don't know. I think I was having some kind of weird dream," she said with a giggle. "Kiss me."

Justin stared down at her another moment. Cynde wrapped her hand around the nape of his neck, pulling his face forward. She kissed him. Justin kissed her back. She could feel that he wanted her and she wrapped her legs around his waist. He pulled his head back again.

"Hey, Cynde…"

"Yeah?"

"I should have asked this before, but… are you on um… do you take uh…"

"Yes," Cynde said with another giggle. "My mom put me on the pill as soon as she heard I was dating a football player."

Justin laughed. "Well…good," he said. "This football player wants some action."

"You got it, champ."

Sixteen

Tuesday, after French, Cynde stopped at her locker on the way to art. As she stacked her books onto the shelf, a small voice came from behind.

"I think this might be yours."

She turned to see Fat Becky, her mouth and lips stained blue from candy. Wrapped in Fat Becky's arms was Cynde's skateboard. Cynde's mouth fell open.

"Found it by the tracks," Fat Becky said. "I woulda brought it in yesterday, but it was really dirty, all covered in mud, so I washed it and then I noticed one of the bearings was coming off, so I—well, I got it replaced for you."

Cynde stood staring at Fat Becky, moved beyond words.

"My cousin skates too," Fat Becky explained. "It didn't cost me nothin."

Cynde took the board from her, set it down to the side, and threw her arms around Fat Becky.

"Oh, my God...thank you so much!" Cynde said, tightly squeezing the hefty girl before releasing her.

"Oh, it's no trouble," Fat Becky said, beaming at Cynde.

"But I never skate to school," Cynde said. "How did you even know it was mine?"

"Well, I remember back in like 6th and 7th grade, you always used to wear a bull necklace," Fat Becky said. "It looked just like the bull painted on the skateboard."

Cynde's mind raced back to the gold bull necklace her father had bought her at a jewelry counter in the Oxford Valley Mall the summer before she'd started 6th grade. It was true; she had worn the necklace every single day for nearly two years.

The night she'd found out her father had cheated on her mother, Cynde had run to the middle of the Calhoun Street Bridge and, in what had felt like a powerful symbolic gesture at the time, she'd hurled the necklace into the Delaware River. She now thought back on it as one of her more childish displays—an embarrassing melodramatic temper tantrum fueled by prepubescent angst and inane notions of love and loyalty.

"Oh, my God..." Cynde said again. "That's quite a memory you have! Thank you so much, F— um Becky."

"It's alright," Fat Becky said. "You can call me 'Fat Becky'," she said. "I know what I am."

Cynde picked up her skateboard and put it into her locker. Fat Becky turned to leave.

"Hey," Cynde said, "You're in my art class, right?"

"Yeah," Fat Becky said. "I sit behind you. I love your drawings. You're so talented."

Cynde had always enjoyed art class, but liked it even more since the regular art teacher, Mrs. Watsoola, had taken a leave of absence early into the first semester, and a substitute named Mr. Krause had taken over the class. He was a slightly built man with light brown hair who looked no older than a high schooler himself. Mr. Krause had taken an interest in Cynde's pencil drawings right away and allowed Cynde to work on them whenever she wanted instead of completing the regular assignments.

"It's art class," he had said. *"That looks like art to me."*

"Wanna walk over with me?" Cynde asked Fat Becky.

"Oh, um...sure," Fat Becky replied.

"Cool." As Cynde slammed her locker closed, she saw Justin jogging up the hall toward her. Quickly, Cynde turned to Fat Becky. "Please don't tell Justin about my skateboard being by the tracks."

Fat Becky nodded solemnly.

"Hey," Justin greeted Cynde, kissing her before noticing Fat Becky. "Hey," he repeated. "Becky, right?"

"Yes," Becky responded shyly.

"Hey," he said again, then turned back to Cynde. "Uh... Coach wants us there immediately after final bell today so, I won't be able to drive you home."

"That's okay. I'll walk," Cynde said, looking to Becky, "Hey. You walk, right? Same direction. Wanna walk with me?"

Becky gaped at her a moment. "Oh, um...sure, I—I can do that."

"Well, actually," Justin interjected, "I asked Zach to drive you home," he said, then glancing at Fat Becky, "I'm sure Zach can drive Becky home too."

Cynde turned to Fat Becky and read the look of terror on the girl's round face.

"No," Cynde told Justin. "No, I'd like to walk today," she said, watching the relief wash over Fat Becky's face.

"Alright," Justin said, leaning in to kiss her cheek again. "I'll let Zach know. I gotta run. Nice to see you, Becky."

***

97

As the girls started down the sidewalk, away from the school, Fat Becky pulled out a handful of blue Jolly Ranchers from her hoodie pocket.

"Want one?" she asked. "Blue's my favorite."

"Okay, thanks," Cynde said, accepting a sugary blue treat.

She knew Fat Becky had a long walk to the Manor, so she invited her to hang out at her house a while. Fat Becky seemed surprised by the invitation, but quickly accepted.

"Beware," Cynde warned as she unlocked the door. "You're about to enter pink hell."

Inside, Fat Becky marveled at the all-pink living room.

"It's… wow… It really is all pink," she said. "It's real pretty though. You have a real nice house."

"Thanks," Cynde said with a laugh. "Want some juice or something?"

"Okay," Fat Becky said, settling on a chair at the kitchen table.

Cynde got out the apple juice and poured two glasses.

"So… how come your skateboard was at the tracks?' Fat Becky asked. "Do you hang out there?"

"No," Cynde replied. "I um… Well, I did go there, but not anymore."

"I know people go back there to drink and do drugs and stuff," Fat Becky said. "I just cut through there to get to and from school faster."

"Oh, you shouldn't," Cynde blurted. "Nothing good ever happens back there," she heard herself say.

"Did something bad happen?"

"No," Cynde said, jumping up and bringing her glass to the sink. "I just know some really shitty people hang out back there."

"I only really know Paul Shale. He hangs out back there with his cousin and some of the older Manor boys." Fat Becky said. "He lives a couple blocks from me."

Cynde felt her stomach churn. "Well, you shouldn't talk to him, Becky. You shouldn't go anywhere near him."

"Why not? Did he try something with you?" she asked. "I actually think he's kinda cute, but I've heard he can get pushy with girls. He never tried nothin' with me though."

Cynde tried to steady her breathing, but she could hear it becoming more ragged. The room started to feel like it was spinning and for a moment, she worried she might vomit. She noticed her hands becoming shaky and tingly just as her vision started turning fuzzy and dark.

> *If I was king, I'd wear a ring*
> *And never hurt my people*
> *I'd stay alert, and dress to kill*
> *I might even slip you something*

"Cynde! Oh, my God, Cynde!"

Cynde found herself lying flat on her kitchen floor with Fat Becky hunched over her. She sat up.

"Are you okay? You smacked your head on the floor pretty hard."

"I'm okay."

Cynde stood up, feeling sweaty and cold and wobbly. She made her way to her bedroom.

"You want me to call someone? Your mom?"

"No. Just come sit with me, okay?"

"Okay."

Cynde sat on the side of the bed. She suddenly felt frightened and began to sob. Fat Becky sat beside her, and wrapped a heavy arm around her. Cynde leaned her head to Fat Becky's chest and cried against her like a child. Fat Becky held Cynde snugly in her arms, rocking her a bit.

"So, I guess something did happen with Paul, huh?" Fat Becky said quietly.

Cynde pulled away from Becky to look in her eyes. "You can never say anything to anyone, okay Becky? Please."

"Oh, no, Cynde, I wouldn't do that to you. Promise," she said. "Do you wanna talk about it?"

Cynde shook her head, then hugged Fat Becky again. "It's nice to have a friend who's a girl," she said. "I haven't had one since I was little."

"What about all them girls at school? They all like you."

"They don't really. I mean, maybe in a way, but for all the wrong reasons."

"Nobody likes me for any reason," said Fat Becky. "Nobody at all even talks to me."

"Well, we can change that," Cynde said, examining Becky.

But Fat Becky wasn't just fat, blue-mouthed, and dressed in old and unfashionable clothing; she was otherwise unfortunate looking too. She had gap teeth, a very wide and kind of flat nose that held a thick pair of glasses in place, oily skin, short, ratty

100

brown hair, and clusters of very noticeable moles on her neck. Cynde realized she couldn't just give Fat Becky a makeover like they would in the movies.

"It's okay. I don't need people to like me," Fat Becky said, sounding resolved. "But it would be nice if we could at least kinda be friends for a little while."

Cynde smiled at Fat Becky. "We'll definitely stay friends, Becky. Maybe even forever."

Fat Becky smiled brightly.

"But Becky," Cynde said, "You have to let Justin drive you home from school from now on, okay?"

Fat Becky's face got that same look of terror as she'd seen before when Justin had suggested Zach drive her home.

"Justin is a really nice person. So is Zach," Cynde continued. "They're not going to judge you. And you're my friend. I don't care where you live. It's not safe to cut under the highway."

She sat staring until Fat Becky gave an uneasy nod.

"Great. So, as soon as Justin gets here, we'll give you a ride home."

Fat Becky gave another uneasy nod.

"Trust me, okay?" Cynde said, holding out her hands. Fat Becky took Cynde's hands. "Friends?"

"Friends," Fat Becky said, still looking nervous but genuinely happy.

***

The girls climbed into Justin's car. In her very small voice from the back seat, Fat Becky directed Justin to her house.

When they arrived, Cynde turned in her seat, "See you tomorrow, Becky."

Becky smiled then looked shyly at Justin. "Thank you for the ride."

"It's no problem at all, Becky," Justin said, smiling warming. "A friend of Cynde's is a friend of mine."

"Thanks, guys," Fat Becky responded quietly.

She opened the door, letting herself out of the back seat and began walking toward a narrow, dilapidated rowhome. There was a short, narrow chain link fence in front of it surrounding a small strip of Astroturf. Cynde could see why Fat Becky had been such a nervous wreck about accepting a ride home. After unlocking and opening her front door, Fat Becky waved to them. Justin and Cynde waved back before Justin turned his car around.

Cynde felt Justin looking at her. She looked up to find him grinning.

"What?" she asked.

"You have a girlfriend!"

"Yeah," Cynde said with a little smile.

"It's nice," he said. "I always thought you hated other girls."

"I don't hate them."

"Well, it's just that... Ya know, a lot of the other girls... They think you're kinda stuck-up because you don't ever really talk to them."

"All those other girls ever want to talk to me about is you. Becky likes *me*."

"Well, it's nice that you've made a friend. But hey, um… How come her mouth is always blue?"

"She likes Jolly Ranchers. The blue ones are her favorite," Cynde explained. "They're actually really good."

"Ah-ha! So that's the secret."

"What?"

"The key to becoming friends with Cynde Ehler: Feed her blue Jolly Ranchers. If only the other girls knew."

Seventeen

Justin and Cynde walked in from the rain. They stood in the alcove, removing their boots and hoodies. Mr. and Mrs. Helvig were both seated in the living room. Mr. Helvig was sorting through a box of receipts and other papers at the desk. Cynde remembered her own father doing that every April. Now, her mother hired an accountant to file her taxes.

Mrs. Helvig was adding new photographs to a family photo album. Cynde's family photo albums hadn't been updated since she was 12 years old.

"Hey, Cynde," Mr. Helvig said as they entered the living room.

"Cynde! It's so nice to see you!" Mrs. Helvig said warmly.

"Nice to see you too, Mrs. Helvig," Cynde said.

"Why don't you two have a seat? I'll bring out some snacks."

"Actually, mom, I'm gonna take Cynde to the den to help her with algebra."

"Smart girl!" Mrs. Helvig said, winking at Cynde.

Cynde smiled.

"Well, you kids go ahead," Mrs. Helvig said. "Dinner will be in about an hour and a half."

***

At dinner, they sat at the family's dining room table. Mrs. Helvig had prepared Cornish hens, asparagus, and fresh baked focaccia. As they ate, Mr. and Mrs. Helvig began discussing details of an upcoming trip. Cynde noticed Justin seemed uncomfortable.

"Justin, are you most of the way packed? I'd just like everyone packed in advance so we don't have to worry the morning of."

"Where um... Where are you going?" Cynde asked quietly.

Mr. Helvig chimed in, "Just for a tour of Penn's campus. Of course, he won't be able to make a decision for a couple weeks, following his tour of my alma mater, Stanford."

Cynde nearly choked on her bite of focaccia. "California?"

She knew the Helvigs were from California. They'd moved to Morrisville when Justin was entering fourth grade. She hadn't ever considered the possibility of Justin returning there for college.

"Yep," Mr. Helvig said. "It's where my grandfather went, where my father went, where I went, and where I met the lovely Mrs. Helvig," he said, smiling at his wife.

"Oh, I wasn't a student there," Mrs. Helvig added shyly. "I was visiting a girlfriend who lived on campus. I was a liberal arts major at Menlo," she said, smiling over at Cynde. "Justin gets his brains from his father."

Cynde looked to Justin.

"It'll just be a tour," Justin said.

"I know, I know. Just a tour," Mr. Helvig interjected, "But that might change once you see Stanford's beautiful campus."

"It's a nice climate out there," Mrs. Helvig added. "Of course, that's about the only thing we miss of California."

Cynde stared down at her plate. "Um... How long will you be gone?" she managed.

"For this trip, we'll leave Saturday, and we should be back early Tuesday evening. We want to stop and see the Mutter Museum and the Rodin Museum, and visit with my sister, Justin's Aunt Miriam, while we're in Philly," she said. "Do you think you might be able to stop by on Sunday, Monday, and Tuesday to feed the angelfish?"

"Oh, um, sure, Mrs. Helvig."

Justin soon excused them from the table and brought Cynde back to his bedroom. Cynde sat on his bed unable to look at Justin, fearing she'd burst into tears. Justin sat beside her.

"Cynde..." he said. "Hey."

The thought of getting through four days without Justin seemed overwhelming to Cynde, but after next year, Justin could be leaving for good. He would be gone, and she'd be alone, or crying in the arms of Fat Becky.

"I have to go," she whispered, standing and walking toward the bedroom door.

"Cynde, no," Justin said, rushing to block the door.

Cynde started to panic, not wanting Justin to see her needy desperation.

"Justin, I really have to go."

"Well, I'm not gonna let you go," he said softly, wrapping his arms around her and drawing her close.

Don't let me go, Justin. Don't ever let me go.

She buried her face in his chest.

"Hey," he said. "Talk to me."

Cynde reached her hand up through Justin's hair, pulling him close, kissing him. He kissed her back, then pulled back to look at her.

"Cynde, I'm not going to Stanford, okay?" he said.

She looked into Justin's face.

"It'll be a tour of the campus. I'm humoring my father. That's all it is."

Cynde nodded, wanting to feel reassured. Justin took her hands and pulled her toward his bed.

"Come here," he said. "Stay with me."

Cynde gratefully slipped into his bed. He moved to lie beside her, wrapping his arm around her. She felt safe in Justin's embrace.

Eighteen

The Helvigs had left for Philadelphia. Cynde made it through Saturday without thinking about what Monday and Tuesday would be like at school without Justin. But by early Sunday afternoon, as she skated to Justin's house to feed his mother's fish, she could feel it creeping into the back of her mind.

Justin's house felt strange without Justin. There were framed photographs of him all over the living room, many of him fishing with his dad and his friend, Zach. She found Mrs. Helvig's note and fed the fish just two pinches per the instructions. Then, she made her way to Justin's room. For a moment, she considered climbing into Justin's bed, wrapping herself snugly into the sweet, delicate fragrance of Justin's sheets. But she knew that would only be a quick fix.

She locked up and got on her skateboard. She didn't know where she was heading, but knew something was out there just waiting for her. She skated onto West Bridge St. She skated past Roger's Safe & Lock Shop, past Borden's Arcade, past Anthony's Pizza, and kept skating until she reached the *Trenton Makes* Bridge.

The walk across the bridge looked inviting. It was a chilly day, and Cynde was glad she'd worn a sweater along with her denim jacket over her patchwork mini dress. She carried her skateboard across the bridge, stopping to stare down at the water a few times. The sky was bright blue, and the Delaware River looked beautiful from overhead. She breathed in deeply, feeling energized. Something was out here for her. She just had to keep going to find it.

She continued across the bridge into Trenton, walking onto New Warren St., then onto Market, and finally onto Barlow. Cynde rarely entered Trenton, but this area was vaguely familiar to her. She remembered coming here once before, although she couldn't remember why. It was the Trenton Transit Station.

She walked into the station and suddenly knew exactly where to go. She walked past the bathrooms, past the ticket sales booths, past the small newsstand, and opened a door on the left. She walked down the stairs, breathing in the smells of cigarette smoke, dust, grease, and something metallic. There was a man sitting on a bench, holding a briefcase on his lap, smoking a cigarette. Otherwise, the platform was empty.

Cynde stood beside a tall lamppost, set her skateboard down, and waited. Passengers began trickling onto the platform until a crowd formed. As the train moved in, she could feel the vibrations in her feet and legs, then rushing throughout her entire body.

The train doors opened. Passengers filed on and off, passing her, walking toward or hurrying from the stairs. She could hear bits and pieces of their conversations. A small group of young men stopped and complimented her looks. She smiled at them, and they moved along. Then it was quiet.

Eventually, more passengers began trickling from the stairs to the platform. Again, Cynde felt the soft rumbles beneath her feet grow into the powerful vibrations that took hold of her body as the next train rushed into the station.

The doors opened. Passengers filed in and out. The doors closed. The train sped away. Quiet. The next train approached. The doors opened. Passengers filed in and out. The doors closed. The train sped away. Quiet.

110

Cynde stood still beside the lamppost, enjoying it all. She loved the sounds, the smells, and the bouts of commotion in between the lulls of quiet. During the next lull, she walked up closer. Staring down from the platform, she stood examining the tracks until the next passengers began trickling in from the stairs. Then, she walked back and took her place beside the lamppost.

After the next train rushed away, she moved up to study the tracks again. When the next passengers began to trickle in, she again returned to her lamppost. This time, as she began to feel the distant rumbling of the train, she moved forward, taking just a couple steps, then a couple steps more.

Suddenly, there was a loud *FWHACK* just beside her, causing her to leap into the air. Startled, she and several other nearby passengers turned to see what had caused the jarring noise. Just a few feet away on the platform, there was a briefcase on its side. Just as she saw it, a man approached her, putting his arm out in front of her.

"I'm not going to touch you, okay?" he said. His voice was deep and firm. "I'm going to take a few steps forward, and you're going to take a few steps back."

Confused, Cynde stared up at the man. He looked angry. Did he work for the train station? Did he think she was trying to ride without a ticket?

"I wasn't going to get on," she tried to explain.

"Step back," the man said sternly.

Cynde stepped backwards until she was standing beside the lamppost again. That's when she recognized the man. He had been sitting on the bench when she'd first entered the platform. He was dressed in a white button-down shirt, dark gray pants and a matching blazer. Had he been sitting there all this time? Puzzled, she continued staring at him. He didn't look angry, she realized. He looked frightened.

"I'm going to put my hand on this lamppost," he said, closing Cynde in with his arm. "When the train arrives, we can sit and talk if you'd like."

He was a tall, trim man, maybe 40, Cynde thought. He had thick, dark hair combed neatly against a fair complexion. His eyes, a steely gray, continued to hold her gaze, not looking away for a second, not blinking. As he stood close to Cynde, she thought she could detect a peppery, powdery smell, maybe an aftershave. She noticed he wore an expensive watch. It looked like the one her father had worn every day. It had been an anniversary gift from Cynde's mother. Cynde had gone with her mother to Macy's to help select it.

Cynde looked up as the train arrived. The man took his arm down from in front of her as passengers began filing in and out of the train.

"Why don't you take a seat?" said the man, gesturing back toward his bench.

"Okay," Cynde agreed, picking up her skateboard and following him.

He stopped and retrieved his briefcase from the platform before sitting. Cynde sat beside him and watched as he reached into the inside breast pocket of his blazer then lit a cigarette with a gold Zippo.

She'd always liked the *clink* sounds of a Zippo lighter opening and closing. Mr. Bauer used a pack of matches he kept tucked into the cellophane around his pack of cigarettes. There was something about a Zippo that seemed so much more composed, more manly than matches. Sexy.

"What's your name?" he asked.

"Cynde."

"Cynde, I'm Gabe."

"Nice to meet you," she said.

"You gave me quite a scare there, Cynde."

"Oh, sorry," Cynde replied.

"You want to talk about what you're doing here?"

"Oh. Well, I just like it here, I guess."

Gabe stared at her silently for what felt like a long time. Cynde began to squirm a bit.

"Hmm," he finally said, taking a long drag of his cigarette. "I do too actually. It's the noise, I think… the commotion… along with the periods of quiet."

"Did you come here just to sit on the platform all day?" Cynde asked incredulously.

Gabe smiled. "I guess you're not the only person here today with a… busy mind."

"Oh. I'm alright," Cynde said.

"I'm glad," said Gabe. "I'm alright too."

Cynde tried to smile.

"So, Cynde, can I buy you a coffee…or a soda?" he asked.

"Juice?"

"After you," Gabe said, gesturing toward the stairs.

Cynde picked up her skateboard. Together, they climbed the stairs.

It was only once she'd re-entered the warmth of the lobby that Cynde realized how cold she was. It seemed strange that she hadn't noticed before. Her hands felt like ice. She shivered, walking with Gabe to the front of the lobby, and got on line at the small snack bar.

"Apple, orange, or cranberry?" he asked.

"Apple, please."

"Alright. Why don't you take a seat at a table?"

She walked to a table by the front window and set her skateboard down. Soon, Gabe approached and sat across from her, holding a coffee, setting an apple juice in front of her.

"Thank you," she said, opening the bottle. The juice was cold and tasted unusually sweet, causing her to shiver more.

"So," Gabe said. "Are you in school?"

"Yes."

"High school?"

"Yes."

"Year?"

"Sophomore."

"That would make you… 16?"

"Almost."

Gabe exhaled noisily. "Well, Cynde... You wanna tell me what's troubling you?"

Cynde felt her bottom lip quivering. Her eyes filled with tears, and she turned her face away to stare out the window. Gabe reached an open hand out to her across the table. Cynde quickly wiped her tears away then turned back, eyeing Gabe's hand. Timidly, she reached out and took it. His fingers closed firmly around her cold hand. His hand was surprisingly warm, and a sudden warmth spread throughout her body.

"Why don't you tell me about it?" he said, giving her hand a light squeeze.

She took her hand away and reached for a napkin to blow her nose.

"Well, it's just that I—I'm all alone," Cynde said.

She looked up, expecting him to reassure her, to tell her she was not alone, that of course there were people who cared about her, that she needed to talk to her parents or perhaps her high school guidance counselor.

But Gabe simply nodded.

"I mean, I guess I'm not all alone yet," Cynde said. "I have a boyfriend. He's really nice."

"Where is he... your boyfriend?"

"Touring a college campus. His father wants him to go to Stanford."

Gabe nodded again.

"He'll leave for college after next year. Then, I'll be alone."

"Some of the most meaningful relationships we have are the fleeting ones. Don't you think?" Gabe asked. "People like to believe the relationships that last are the ones that matter. It's nice to believe that. But it's not true… not really. The people who stay are the ones we rely on for whatever it is we need, but it's the ones who rush in and out of our lives who tell us our story and show us who we are as we catch a glimpse of who they are." He took a sip of his coffee. "They bring some excitement or at least a little something to think about, and then they leave us with our thoughts and sometimes a little pain."

"That's kind of a sad thought." Cynde said.

"Yeah," Gabe said. "But maybe sadness doesn't matter… because happiness isn't the point."

"So… what *is* the point?" Cynde asked.

Gabe stared back at Cynde as she eagerly awaited his insight. But he only shrugged.

"Can I give you a lift somewhere?" he asked.

"I live just over the bridge. Morrisville."

"Alright. Wait inside. I'll go get my car and pull it around. It's a black Jeep Cherokee."

Gabe left the table and continued toward the front entrance. Cynde carried her skateboard to stand by the door and waited. After a few minutes, Gabe pulled up and gave a single motion wave from the window of his Jeep Cherokee. Cynde carried her skateboard out and got into his passenger seat.

He drove quietly. From the corner of her eye, Cynde kept watch of Gabe's hands. He mostly steered with his left hand, his right intermittently assisting but mostly resting in his lap. Whenever he turned the wheel, he'd let his fingers lightly graze

116

over it until the wheel reached its centered position. Cynde imagined what his fingers might feel like grazing across her skin that way, again noticing the smell of his aftershave. As he drove across the bridge, Cynde stole a glimpse of his face, his eyes locked on the road ahead. She noticed his jaw clenching a bit.

Once over the bridge, Cynde directed him to her house. He pulled his car over just out front and put it into park.

"Do you want to come in?" Cynde asked. "No one's home. No one will be home for hours."

"Uh… no," Gabe said. "No, thank you. I need to get going."

"Okay," Cynde said. "Well, thank you."

"You're very welcome, Cynde. I want you to take care of yourself, okay?"

"Okay," she said.

She stared a moment longer. Finally, she closed her eyes and leaned her face in to kiss him. She felt Gabe take hold of her chin, stopping her. She opened her eyes to find his steely eyes staring back, causing a stir deep inside her. Then, he turned her face away and kissed her cheek. He brought his other hand up to hold her face and again brushed his lips against her cheek. He pressed his face to the side of hers, and she could hear his breathing grow heavy. He gently kissed her cheek once more then released her.

"You take care of yourself, Cynde," he repeated.

Cynde looked once more into his steely eyes. He stared back, then gave her a gentle smile. She smiled back.

"Okay," she said.

She picked up her skateboard, opened the door, and got out. Gabe remained parked in place until she unlocked her front door and turned back. He gave her a single motion wave goodbye and drove off.

Nineteen

Cynde microwaved a Swanson frozen meal for dinner. She showered and slipped into her babydoll pajamas, then climbed into bed early.

She thought of Gabe's Zippo, the clinking sound it made. She thought of his fingers grazing the steering wheel as it turned, his steely eyes staring back at hers, his lips pressed against her cheek, his heavy breathing, the smell of cigarettes and aftershave. She reached her hand down between her thighs. She thought of Justin on top of her, inside her, but her mind began to race.

She rolled onto her side, trying to sleep. After a few minutes, the phone began to ring. She made her way back to the dark kitchen and picked up the receiver.

"Hello?"

"Cynde!" Justin exclaimed. "I've tried you a bunch of times today. How are you?"

"Oh, I'm okay," Cynde said. "How are you?"

"Missing my girl. What did you do today?"

"Not too much. I fed your mother's fish, then skated around town a bit. How's Penn?"

"Really nice," he said. "Listen, do me a favor?"

"Sure, what?"

"We'll be home Tuesday...early evening. When I get home, I'd really like to find you waiting for me, in my bed. Can you be there, waiting for me?"

Cynde smiled into the phone. "Yeah, I can do that."

"Great. I'm looking forward to it already," he said. "I've gotta go. I'm on my parent's hotel bill. I miss you, Cynde."

"I miss you too, Justin."

After hanging up the phone, Cynde went back to bed with a renewed sense of hope. Maybe she and Justin would find a way. She liked picturing a future with Justin. She liked imagining herself lying in his bed all day like a doll that only comes to life with his touch.

***

Cynde woke late. Monday morning felt even more miserable than usual, knowing she would be walking to school alone. Her mother hadn't come home, so she brushed her hair into loose pigtails. She dressed in a pair of baggy jeans and her white *Hard Tail* half-top, adding Justin's blue and white flannel shirt that she'd swiped from him. As she rolled up the sleeves so they wouldn't hang, she was disappointed to notice the flannel no longer smelled like Justin. Still, the soft fabric added a layer of warmth and somehow felt a bit like armor. As she walked to school, she thought through Justin's wardrobe, wondering what she might borrow next.

By the time she finally entered the building, first period was already halfway over. The office receptionist wrote her a pass and assigned her an after-school detention.

"Get there by 3:05," she warned.

Cynde stopped in the girls' bathroom. A few girls had been chattering at the mirror as she walked in but fell into a hushed silence as she entered. She approached the mirror to check her reflection and smooth on a coat of cherry lip gloss, feeling the girls continue to stare at her. They always stared at her. The difference was the silence. She guessed they'd heard Justin was touring college campuses and were hoping to see her cry.

Vultures.

She made her way to class.

"Thank you for fitting us into your tight schedule, Cynde," Mr. Bauer said.

"It ain't that tight!" someone shouted. The class laughed.

What the fuck?

During class, she saw students passing notes and could hear them whispering. She couldn't make out anything, but knew they were talking about her. She started to feel a bit uneasy, but by the end of history, she'd decided to brush it off. On her way to French, Kathy Jacobs approached her in the hall. She had a new giant zit right at the center of her forehead. It was very red and caked in foundation. Cynde tried not to stare at it.

"So, is it true?" Kathy asked.

"Is what true?"

"Did you actually fuck Paul Shale?"

Suddenly feeling as though she'd had the wind knocked out of her, Cynde reached out and gripped the water fountain.

"What?"

"Yeah. Fat Becky told everyone you fucked Paul Shale back by the tracks," Kathy said. "So, did ya?"

"Becky?"

Just then, she noticed Fat Becky watching her from the end of the hall. Fat Becky quickly averted her eyes and swerved out of sight. Cynde leaned back against the wall, worried she might faint. She thought of Justin's face right after he'd caught her with Luke.

Justin…

Struggling to breathe, she slowly slumped to the floor.

"Oh, my God, Cynde… Ew!" Kathy squealed. "Did you?! Did you actually do it?!"

"Leave me alone," Cynde managed to get out.

She knew Kathy had said more after that, but she wasn't sure what. She felt a crowd of students watching her as the hallway filled with cacophonous gossip and laughter. Cynde rested her face in her hands.

> *The wash is out, it's hanging up*
> *And all I have is nothing*
> *Nothing to do, nothing to say*
> *I think I must be dreaming*

She wasn't sure how long she'd been bent into her lap, but when she finally managed to lift her head, the hallway was empty and suddenly felt eerily quiet.

She climbed to her feet and walked to French class where she was lectured in French about tardiness, and the whispering continued. Cynde didn't actually care much about what other people thought. But every time she pictured Justin, her stomach would churn and her hands would start to shake.

"Cynde? Comment allez-vous aujourd'hui?"

"Je vais tres bien aujourd'hui."

"Quel temps fait-il aujourd'hui?"

"Le temps est frais aujourd'hui."

"Est-ce qu'il pleut?"

"Non, il ne pleut pas."

"Est-ce qu'il fait beau?"

"Oui, il fait beau."

"Tres bien, mademoiselle. Fille intelligente!"

It had been Cynde's mother's idea for her to study French. Cynde thought it was a ghastly sounding language, but her mother had promised to take her on a trip to Paris if she'd stuck with it her first year.

"You'll be glad to speak the language when you meet a young handsome Frenchman in a cafe," she recalled her mother telling her, insisting French men were *"witty, charming, and utterly irresistible."*

The argument had been a compelling one at the time, and Cynde had taken her studies very seriously. Only, once she'd gotten to Paris, she found that French men seemed just a bit too much like women. The trip had been fun and interesting nonetheless, but she'd been grateful to return home to the land of real and truly irresistible men. That was the summer before 8th grade. Now, she just stuck with French for the easy elective credit.

By the time class had ended, Cynde was distracted and feeling a bit more stable. She managed to tune out the other students in the hall, and took her seat in art class, doubting Fat Becky would have the nerve to show up.

Cynde didn't know why Fat Becky had done what she'd done —why she'd rescued and returned her skateboard in what had seemed a supreme act of kindness only to try to destroy her later. She'd probably never really know.

123

Fat Becky did show up to art, and she sat directly behind Cynde as usual. Cynde could feel her face growing hot with a strange combination of rage, shame, and a little heartache, but she refused to let herself turn around to acknowledge Fat Becky, instead throwing herself into her new drawing: the face of a man with steely gray eyes.

At lunch, Cynde wandered the halls, deciding only in the last few minutes to get on line at the cafeteria to buy herself an Arctic Splash iced tea. When she arrived, she was stunned to see Kathy Jacobs and the other girls sitting with Fat Becky.

Fat Becky looked so out of place among all the cute, stylish, popular girls, sitting there all fat and blue-mouthed in her old, ugly clothing. Cynde nearly laughed out loud at the sight. That's when Paul Shale walked by, giving her a quick wink.

"Hey, alien face."

Twenty

Detention was mostly quiet. Coach Gevin handed Cynde a book.

"The A section of the glossary," he said wincing. "Sorry."

Cynde found it absurd that they'd always have her copy the A section of the glossary in detention. Why not move through the alphabet? Surely, there would be some benefit to making one's way through the entire glossary over repeating the A section again and again. But she knew it wasn't Coach Gevin's call, so she only smiled at him and began writing:

Aardvark: A burrowing mammal (Orycteropus afer) of sub-Saharan Africa, having a stocky body, large ears, a long tubular snout, and powerful digging claws for feeding on ants and termites.

Cynde hated spending any more time at school than absolutely necessary, but at least she wouldn't have to see Fat Becky walking home with Kathy Jacobs & co. She already decided she would be skipping school tomorrow. Justin would be home tomorrow night, and although it would probably be their last night together, she planned to enjoy it.

She would wait in Justin's bed all day long tomorrow. When he got home, she would give herself to him one last time, make passionate love to him all night long. In the morning, he would drive her to school and then likely never speak a word to her again. She knew she would have to deal with the heartbreak, the desperate longing, the loneliness. But first, she'd have one last perfect night.

Cynde got up around 8 AM. She showered and dressed in her denim miniskirt and black tank top, brushed her hair into pigtails and pulled on her black plastic tattoo choker. She was about to scoot out the door and head over to Justin's when she saw Officer Gallo crawling by in his cruiser.

Damn. I'll never make it 10 blocks without him catching me.

She realized she'd have to sit tight until after school hours. She painted her fingernails and toenails with her mother's taupe nail polish, let it dry, then sat at the kitchen table with her drawing pad.

She waited until 3:15 to leave the house, and had just made it down her front walk to the sidewalk when Luke pulled up in his Land Rover. He slowly rolled along the side of the road as she continued walking.

"Cynde! Hey c'mon, I just wanna talk. Cynde!"

"Luke, please, I need to get somewhere."

"Let me drive you."

"No, I want to walk."

"Cynde, please. Just get in. Just talk to me, okay? Please. Just talk."

Cynde glanced over at him nervously.

"Just talk," he repeated, holding his hands up.

She walked over to his car, still eyeing Luke. Luke looked back, his hands held up in place. She opened the door and climbed into his passenger seat.

"Thank you," he said, shifting into park and rolling up the window.

"Luke, I just—"

"I left Elise," he said, cutting her off.

Elise.

Cynde knew Luke had been with her for 10 years, since his senior year of high school, but it was the first time she had heard the woman's name.

"I need you back, Cynde. This isn't what you think," he said. "I really care about you."

"Luke, I'm—"

"I know, you're... younger, but this isn't me being some fucked-up perv trying to score a piece of teenage ass, okay?" he said. "Cynde, I love you."

It was the first time any man other than her father had said those words to her. She'd always wondered what it would feel like. Strangely, it didn't feel like much.

"You're just so... pure, Cynde."

"Pure?"

"Pure," he repeated. "I don't know. It's just so different with you," he said. "I can't even say where things started to get fucked up with Elise, but it was long before I even met you. I just hadn't fully realized it. We used to like each other—*really* like each other...at least I think we did. But eventually, it was like...I don't know, I wasn't enough. And I tried to step up my game, but little by little, I was just...trading my integrity...changing my whole fucking identity to conform to this tiny little part in the big package deal she's looking for. " He paused, rubbing his eyes with the palms of his hands, then running his fingers up through his hair. He looked back at Cynde. "With you, I never had to be anyone but me."

Cynde stared blankly.

"I need you back, Cynde. I need you back," he said, reaching for her.

Cynde awkwardly patted his shoulder as he embraced her. He turned toward her and pressed his lips to hers. She quickly turned her face away.

"No, Luke."

He pulled her face back toward him and forcefully continued kissing her, holding her tightly in his arms. After a minute, he moved down to her neck, kissing just below her ear.

"Luke, stop."

"Oh, God, Cynde. Don't you remember how special it was with us?" he moaned into her ear. "I need you back. Come back to me. Let me take you to my place. We can start fresh."

"Luke, please…"

"I need to feel you," he panted against her face.

Luke raised his hand, stuck his index and middle fingers into his mouth then reached them down between her thighs. Cynde squeezed her legs together, but he forced his hand between them and began digging his fingers into the side of her underwear.

"No, Luke, please stop!"

She tried to pull the car door open, but that small shift in the passenger seat only assisted him, and Luke pushed his fingers inside her.

Tears now running down her face, Cynde wailed. The sound seemed to jolt Luke to attention. He suddenly froze, staring at her, first with a look of confusion, then horror.

"Oh, God, what am I doing?" he breathed out. He removed his fingers and pulled back. "Oh, God, Cynde, I'm so sorry. I don't know what just happened to me. I'm so sorry."

Cynde sat, sobbing for a minute. Soon, she collected herself and opened the passenger door.

"Cynde, I'm sorry. Oh, God, I'm so sorry. Cynde, please forgive me. I'm so fucking sorry."

She got out and slammed the door closed. Luke continued calling out to her, apologizing again and again as she wiped away her tears and started walking down the street. Eventually, she heard Luke turn his car around and drive away.

Twenty-One

Cynde had walked a couple blocks when she heard Weezer's "Only In Dreams" playing from an approaching car stereo.

"Hey, Cynde! Hop in!"

She turned to see Zach in his 1985 blue Lincoln Town Car. Zach Camphire had moved to Morrisville with his father the summer before his fifth grade year, just after his mother had died of cancer. He and Justin had become fast friends, and Zach had practically lived with the Helvigs throughout his middle school years. Now, he and Justin were the two star players of the high school football team.

Zach and Justin were similar heights and builds. Zach had a pronounced brow ridge over green-flecked hazel eyes that always looked serious but were offset by his easy smile and soft blonde hair, cut in the same floppy style as Justin's.

"Hey, Zach," Cynde said, getting into his car.

"Are you headed to Justin's? He's not home yet, is he?"

"No, he'll be home tonight. I'm going over to feed Mrs. Helvig's fish. Then, I'll probably just sit around and wait for him.

"Cool, cool," Zach said. "Justin will be very glad to see you when he gets in." He took a deep breath, lowering the volume on his car stereo. "So...uh...that rumor...."

Cynde winced.

"Obviously, I know it isn't true," Zach said. "I'll never understand why you girls can't just play nice."

Cynde kept quiet.

"Well, you don't have to worry about it anymore," Zach continued. "Everyone knows it isn't true."

"They didn't yesterday."

"Well, today, Paul Shale told everyone it isn't true."

"He did?"

"Yup. So, it's dead. Alright?" Zach said, parking in front of Justin's house, turning off Weezer. He turned toward her. "Do me a favor though, Cynde, okay?" he asked. "Clear it with Justin before school tomorrow. I swear to you it's dead, but still, catching wind of this sort of thing secondhand could really mess a guy up, ya know?"

"Zach," Cynde said, feeling tears returning to her eyes. "I don't know how to... I mean, I just don't know what to say," she cried.

"Hey, hey," Zach said, resting a hand on her shoulder. "Don't worry about it, okay? Don't worry about it. You just give our boy a nice warm homecoming, and I'll be sure to get at him first thing tomorrow morning."

Cynde looked up nervously into Zach's deep, serious eyes.

"Like it never happened, Cynde. Promise."

"Okay," Cynde said, wiping her eyes.

"Hey, um...Cynde," Zach continued, patting her shoulder, then cupping it a bit more firmly. "Listen, I need to ask you a question, okay? Did Paul Shale... ya know, did he... put his hands on you?"

Cynde shook her head vigorously, "No."

Zach continued staring at her for a while, saying nothing. Cynde looked away, beginning to squirm under his intense gaze, then finally stared back into Zach's eyes.

"Okay. Done," he said, releasing her shoulder. "Justin. First thing tomorrow morning, okay? I got this."

"Okay."

"Take good care of my boy, alright?" Zach said with a smile. "He's crazy about you, ya know."

Cynde smiled. "Thanks, Zach."

As soon as she entered the house, she fed Mrs. Helvig's angelfish then went to Justin's room. She looked through his CD collection, found Weezer's Blue Album, and put it on loop. Then, she went to Justin's closet, swiped his gray and white flannel and put it on. She stretched out atop his bed, breathing in his smell, listening to Weezer until she fell asleep.

**

"Hey," she heard Justin's voice saying just above Weezer's "No One Else." She felt him nuzzling her face. "You're here," he said.

Opening her eyes, she saw the sun was setting outside. She turned toward Justin, smiling. "Blue Album, huh?" he said. "Good call."

He kissed her.

"Zach had it playing in his car," she said, groggily.

"Mmmm…" he moaned, kissing her again. "Good call, Zach."

"I'm so glad you're home," Cynde said. "I missed you."

133

"I missed you too. I don't like being away from you so long."

Twenty-Two

Justin had dropped Cynde home around 6:45 AM, giving her an hour to shower and change for school. When she got out of the shower, her mother was sitting on her bed.

"Hey, ma."

"Cynde, if you're going to be out all night, would you please leave a note?"

"Okay."

"How's Justin?"

"Fine. Picking me up again for school soon."

"Braids?"

"Yes, please."

Cynde dressed in her baggy camo pants and fitted white *Girl Skateboard* t-shirt with the bright green logo at the center. She applied a coat of cherry lip gloss, then waited on her front steps.

As always, Justin was right on time. He was wearing jeans and his soft gray sweater over a white t-shirt.

"I like this," Cynde said, petting the sleeve of his sweater.

"Yeah?"

"Yeah."

"You're not getting it," he said.

"What?"

"What?" he repeated in his mock girl voice. "You have my blue hoodie, my gray hoodie, my brown leather jacket, my letterman jacket, at least three of my t-shirts, my blue and white flannel, and now my gray and white flannel," he said, pulling her against him, kissing her neck. "You know I don't mind sharing, but if I let you continue to raid at this rate... I'll soon be naked," he sang.

Cynde laughed. Justin pulled her close again, kissing her.

"You can hold onto the letterman jacket, but return the rest," he said. "Then you can borrow this sweater."

Cynde gave him an exaggerated pout. Justin kissed her forehead and began driving. Cynde held Justin's hand as he drove, nervously wondering if Zach would be able to get to Justin before anyone else did.

Relief washed over her as soon as they drove up to the school. Zach was standing right out front on the sidewalk, his floppy blonde hair shining in the sunlight. He offered a single nod as Justin pulled in.

The moment Justin parked, Nicolette Lamont approached Zach, slipping her arms around him beneath his black leather jacket. Nicolette was a cute blonde cheerleader and friends with Kathy Jacobs.

Interference!

Cynde felt her nerves coming back. Justin turned to her.

"I'll stop over to see you after first period," he said. "I should probably catch up with Zach before school. Okay?"

"Of course," she said, smiling and leaning in to kiss Justin.

They got out of the car, and Cynde made her way to the first set of stairs. She turned and looked back as she climbed them. Zach had managed to extricate himself from Nicolette and now had his arm slung over Justin. Cynde watched as Zach patted Justin's shoulder a few times before cupping it in his hand, steering Justin over toward the side of the building.

Cynde took a deep breath and continued walking. She made her way into the building before first bell and walked straight into the girls bathroom.

"Cynde!" Kathy Jacobs exclaimed. It looked like she'd managed to pop the zit at the center of her forehead. It was now flat and scabbed over but still caked in makeup. Otherwise, Kathy's face looked a bit clearer than usual. Cynde wondered if she'd started using *Proactiv.* "Hey. Sorry about the other day. I mean, I know that was dumb, listening to Fat Becky. And ew… like you'd ever fuck Paul Shale."

Cynde tried to smile at Kathy as she pulled her tube of cherry lip gloss out of her backpack.

"Oh, my God," she continued. "Did you *hear* about Paul?"

"I did!" Colleen Diblin chimed in. Colleen was wearing at least a dozen pink and white glittery mini butterfly clips in her short red hair. Cynde wondered if Colleen regretted the pixie cut and was now trying to doll it up in order to avoid looking butch. "He got the fuck beat outta him!"

"What?" Cynde asked.

"Yup!" Kathy said. "They found him laying in the mud back by the tracks, all fucked up. Like, we're not gonna be seeing him for a while."

Cynde felt her mouth fall open and quickly pivoted to enter one of the stalls.

"I heard one of his hands was totally crushed," someone said.

"Gallo told my dad he was found unconscious. Apparently, he has a concussion, eyes were all swollen shut, and there was a big fuckin goose egg on his forehead," someone else said.

"Who fucked him up?" Cynde heard another girl ask.

"I dunno. Heard he ain't talkin," Colleen answered. "Who the fuck knows with them Manor boys."

Cynde locked the stall door. Her heart was pounding, her hands trembling. Her breathing had turned ragged as she tried to steady herself, leaning back against the door. She dropped her backpack to the floor and reached a hand down the front of her pants, inhaling deeply.

> *You can't avoid her*
> *She's in the air*
> *In between molecules*
> *Of oxygen and carbon dioxide*

Her toes curled inside her combat boots then released, her body quivering against the locked stall door.

Cynde slipped her hand back out, flushed the toilet, and unlocked the door. She returned to the mirror, noticing her cheeks were just a bit flushed, and smiled at her reflection. She washed her hands with the pink liquid soap, drying them on her pants, and leaving the bathroom. As she stepped out into B hall, she realized she wasn't sure if Kathy and the other girls had still been talking to her or not.

"...a lot of the other girls...they think you're kinda stuck-up because you don't ever really talk to them."

138

For a second, Cynde thought about turning back, but first bell rang.

Eh. Fuck 'em.

***

After history, Justin was waiting for her outside the classroom door. Nervously, she packed up her books and made her way over to him.

"Hey," he said, taking her hand. "I need to talk to you. I'll walk you to French."

"Okay," Cynde said quietly.

"Zach tells me you had some trouble with the girls while I was gone."

"Um...yeah."

"Well, I know you don't let gossip get to you, but I think you actually liked that Becky girl, so I'm sorry to hear she stabbed you in the back," Justin said. "That sucks."

"Yeah."

"So, anyway," he said, stopping in the middle of the hall, pulling Cynde against him. "I need to ask you something."

She was trapped. She could feel her heart begin to race.

"How do feel about sharing a car with Zach and Nicolette for Spring Fling?"

"What?"

"Well, I think it'd be nice. I know my mom would love to get pictures of Zach and me together, but I don't know how you feel about Nicolette," he said.

"Like it never happened, Cynde. Promise."

"So, do you hate her?" Justin asked. "She wasn't one of the girls spreading the stupid rumor, was she?"

"Oh!" Cynde said, "Oh, no, I don't think so. I don't really know Nicolette, but she seems like a nice girl."

"Zach thinks so," Justin said. "Can I tell them we'll share a car for Spring Fling?"

"Absolutely," Cynde smiled. "Whatever Zach wants."

Twenty-Three

On Saturday afternoon, Mrs. Helvig decided to take Cynde dress shopping. She'd encouraged Cynde to invite her mother along, but Cynde hadn't bothered. She'd simply find the dress with Mrs. Helvig then get the money from her mother to pay for it.

Cynde knew formal dances were things teenage girls were supposed to get excited about. She knew she should be racking her brain, trying to imagine perfect cuts, colors, styles, and corsages, but the whole idea just struck Cynde as a silly waste of time.

Dances were for girls who wanted to get dressed up, ride in a limo, get their pictures taken with their dates, and pretend it all meant something important enough to justify losing their virginity. She couldn't really see the point in her attending such an event at all, except that she knew Justin wanted to take her, and maybe even more so, Justin's mother wanted to help her prepare.

They were nearly to the store Mrs. Helvig had selected. It was on the Boulevard in Northeast Philly. She'd insisted it was the first place to look. Cynde hoped it was the only place they'd have to look.

"Are you planning to wear your hair up or down?" Mrs. Helvig asked.

"Oh. Um. I'm not sure. What do you think?"

"Well, you have such thick, beautiful hair. I'm thinking it would look very elegant swept into an updo with some gentle curls hanging down, maybe just a bit of baby's breath tucked into it here and there. Of course, you also have the length for a high braided crown, or a half crown if you wanted to leave it partway down. I could have my stylist take a look."

Cynde turned to examine Mrs. Helvig's soft, bouncy, blonde hair as she had many times before and wondered how often Mrs. Helvig saw a stylist. Her own mother had begun going every month when Cynde was around 9, often dragging Cynde with her. She remembered when her father had begun complaining about the unnecessary expense. It was something he'd never seemed to mind until very suddenly near the end.

"Okay," Cynde agreed.

Mrs. Helvig turned to smile at her. "Have you thought of what colors you'd like to try on today?"

"Um…"

"Well, your complexion is quite fair, but with your natural glow, and the dark hair, and that perfect little figure, I was thinking you might like to try something in white."

"White?"

"Off-white?" she quickly suggested. "Cream? Maybe an alabaster. Oh, or maybe ivory!" she added with a cheerful little clap.

Cynde wasn't sure she knew what any of those words meant, other than white.

"You know," Mrs. Helvig continued, "It just might help Justin to imagine the not-so-distant future."

"Oh, um…"

"Well, it's not as though I'm trying to rush anything," she said. "It's just that… it would be nice for Justin to imagine a future… here… with you. Wouldn't it?"

Cynde sat quietly a moment, putting together what Mrs. Helvig was saying.

"Oh, well, sure, Mrs. Helvig," Cynde said. "But I'm pretty sure Justin's planning to go to Princeton or Penn. And I really doubt my dress would change anything otherwise."

"Has he told you that?" she asked, her eyes wide with hope. "Princeton or Penn?"

"Well, he told me he's not going to Stanford," Cynde said, adding, "I'm not sure I was supposed to repeat that."

Mrs. Helvig drew a deep breath and exhaled noisily, then pantomimed locking her lips and throwing away the key.

"Oh, well, that's just…" Mrs. Helvig said, swallowing. "That's just so wonderful to hear."

She turned into the dress store parking lot, parked, then sat back a moment, her eyes closed.

"Are you okay, Mrs. Helvig?"

"Oh, yes," she breathed out, smiling at Cynde. "You have no idea what a relief this is to me. It's not easy to watch your only child grow up," she said, pausing and looking downward. "I know his father wants him to go to Stanford, but… well, the thought of Justin moving so far away…" she trailed off, looking back up at Cynde. "Of course, you won't say anything about this to Mr. Helvig."

Cynde pantomimed locking her lips and throwing away the key.

"Well, let's go find you a dress!" She said smiling brightly.

Cynde tried on many dresses—short ones, long ones, red ones, yellow ones, purple ones, and even a teal one at the shop girl's insistence: *"You'd be crazy not to bring out those eyes of yours!"* But Cynde felt certain that no one would ever manage to overlook her eyes.

Ultimately, Mrs. Helvig had fallen in love with a floor length ballgown with an open back and a square neckline. She'd referred to the color as "champagne," insisting there were undertones of pink and gold, but Cynde was pretty sure it was white. She guessed Mrs. Helvig still hadn't managed to rid herself of the fear of losing Justin, which Cynde could certainly understand. She agreed it was the one she'd have her mother purchase, but Mrs. Helvig insisted on paying for it on the spot, and having it tailored for a perfect fit right away.

"I couldn't have asked for a better child than Justin, of course, but I've always thought it would be nice to have a daughter for these kinds of occasions. It's an absolute joy for me to buy you this dress," she said. "Besides, the dance is coming up in only a little over two weeks. We don't want to take any chances."

"Thank you, Mrs. Helvig," Cynde said. "That's very kind of you."

"You know, Cynde," Mrs. Helvig said once they got back to the car, "You could call me Sabrina. I'd like it if you would."

"Okay. Sabrina," Cynde repeated with a smile.

They spent the rest of the afternoon sitting in a local coffee shop, looking through magazines, discussing hairstyles and corsages. Mrs. Helvig decided a white rose with greens wrist corsage and matching boutonniere would be best. *"Simple but elegant,"* she'd said. Cynde didn't have an opinion about any of it and was glad to have Mrs. Helvig to make the selections. Cynde liked to think of a future with Mrs. Helvig as her mother-in-law. It would be nice to have a woman like her around.

Twenty-Four

It was Tuesday night, the night before Justin was scheduled to tour the Princeton campus. Mr. and Mrs. Helvig had decided they'd leave early the next morning and make a day of it, which meant Cynde would be feeding the angelfish again since they didn't plan to get back until late Wednesday evening.

She and Justin sat at her kitchen table with her algebra homework. Justin was patient as usual, but Cynde was distracted and kept making mistakes.

"Can't we just skip the rest of this?" she asked.

"No, let's finish it," Justin said, standing behind and leaning over her.

She could feel him breathing right next to her ear and turned to kiss him. He tried to pull away, but she grabbed the back of his head, pressing his face to hers and stood up. She wrapped her arms around Justin's waist and pressed her breasts against him. Justin groaned against her mouth but then pulled his head back.

"C'mon, Cyn. It's three more problems. Let's just knock 'em out."

Cynde could feel his erection pressing against her abdomen and wiggled against it.

"I know you want me as much as I want you," she whispered.

"More," he said back. "And just as soon as you finish your math homework, I'll get to have you."

She pressed further into him.

"Sit down," he said firmly.

She released a short frustrated growl and sat back down. Justin leaned back over her, pointing at the page.

"I think you forgot to use the Distributive Property here," he said softly.

It took every last ounce of willpower Cynde had, but she finally managed to absorb Justin's explanations and complete her algebra assignment.

***

They slept naked in each other's arms until 5 AM. Justin had agreed to be ready to leave for Princeton by 7.

"So, Princeton…" Cynde said, running her fingers over his chest. "Like a half hour away?"

"About that, yeah," he answered.

"Would you live on campus?"

"I don't see why I'd do that."

"Maybe to have the full college experience."

"What, like frat parties?" Justin asked.

Cynde shrugged.

"Is that really how you see me?" he asked.

"No."

"So?"

"Maybe you'll meet a really pretty, smart girl."

"I have a really pretty, smart girl."

Go ahead. Say something smart, smart girl.

"You'll be sick of me by then. She'll be fresh and exciting."

Justin laughed.

"It's true," Cynde said. "Men like variety."

"Did you read that in a magazine?"

Cynde turned away from him. Justin pulled her onto her back, pinning her torso with his.

"Cynde," he began, "I know you know me better than this."

"Do I?"

Justin took a deep breath. "What do I eat for breakfast every morning?"

"A hamburger patty."

"Do you know why?"

"Because you're a freak?"

"Well, maybe," he said. "But it's also because one morning, when I was in the second grade, my mother served runny eggs for breakfast."

"You hate runny eggs."

"That's right, I do" he said. "But my mother had read an article about how Americans were guilty of overcooking eggs. Apparently, the French serve scrambled eggs that are a creamy, custard-like texture and, according to the author, cooking them any more than that is uncivilized."

Utterly irresistible runny-egg-eating girlboys

149

"Well, being one of those uncivilized Americans, I refused to eat that morning. My mother tried preparing her regular scrambled eggs. She tried getting me to eat just the toast and sausage. But those French-style scrambled eggs had turned my stomach enough that I wouldn't eat a bite of anything she tried to feed me, until she fried up a hamburger patty... which I ate. And I decided that would be my breakfast from then on."

"What?!"

"Yup."

"You've eaten hamburgers for breakfast—"

"Every day since the second grade. Yes."

Cynde stared in disbelief.

"I don't know why this surprises you," Justin said. "You steal all my clothes. What can you tell me about them?"

"Your clothes? They're big, and warm, and they smell like you."

He smiled and kissed her.

"I'm glad you enjoy them, but I still want them back," he said, repositioning himself in between her legs. "Anyway, surely, you've noticed that all my clothes are—?" he paused expectantly.

"Gray, blue, and white?"

"Well, yeah, that too, I guess," he said. "But they're all Levi Strauss."

"They are?"

"Yup. Every t-shirt, every hoodie, every sweater, every flannel. Levi Strauss."

"I never noticed."

"Thankfully, you don't steal my jeans, but they're all Levi's too. So are my boxers."

"But why?"

"Because I find what I like, and I stick with it," he said, gently thrusting into her.

She inhaled sharply, lifting her legs up around him.

"I love you, Cynde."

The words seemed to reverberate through her entire body. Her head felt fuzzy. Her face, ears, and neck grew warm and a little prickly. Her fingers and toes tingled. She wrapped her arms tightly around him.

"I love you, Justin."

Twenty-Five

Cynde had floated through her morning. She'd worn a long flowy button down black dress with a white polkadot print, and as the fabric swept against her legs, she couldn't help but think about the ballgown Mrs. Helvig had selected for her. She found herself unexpectedly excited thinking about how Justin would look in a suit. Smiling to herself, she walked through B hall to the art room. Right away, she saw that the desks had been rearranged in a circle.

"Change of scenery today," Mr. Krause announced. "It's art class. Why keep the room stagnant?" Then, with a chuckle, he added, "Actually, the janitor moved the desks around, and I didn't feel like moving them back."

Cynde took a seat toward the far end of the circle, pulling out her case of pencils and sketch pad. As she began to sketch, Fat Becky entered the room, sitting at a desk close to the door, almost directly across from Cynde. Cynde noticed right away that Fat Becky's mouth wasn't blue. Today, her mouth was stained a putrid shade of green instead.

She must've run out of the blues.

Cynde turned to a fresh page in her sketchpad and began a new drawing. Furiously, she sketched out a big round face with a heavy double chin, and a thick pair of glasses resting on a wide, flat nose. She regularly glanced up at Fat Becky who was painting today's watercolor assignment, her green tongue partially hanging from her green mouth. Cynde topped the head with frizzy, ratty hair, then added a thick neck covered in clusters of moles. She drew gapped teeth with a meaty tongue lazily hanging out.

Finally, she dropped her gray pencil back in its case and lifted out the blue one to color in the center of the lips and tongue, adding just a faint blue tint to the teeth. By the time she was finished, the period was nearly over. Cynde put her blue pencil down and shook out her cramping hand.

"Astounding!" Mr. Krause's voice said from over her shoulder. "A remarkable likeness," he said, then gave a little laugh. "I hope your subject approves." He laughed again, drawing the attention of the other students who came over to look at Cynde's work.

There were many loud gasps followed with whispering and snickering. Soon, the entire class was on their feet, standing behind Cynde, roaring with laughter as they stared directly across the circle at Fat Becky. Fat Becky sat squirming the few minutes before the bell rang. Then, she stood up and carried her watercolor to dry on the back counter, passing by Cynde to glance down at the likeness of her own hideous face. Without a word, she continued back to her desk, collected her items and left the room.

Cynde wasn't sure how she felt as other students continued to congratulate her on her drawing of a blue-mouthed Fat Becky. She tried to smile back at them, but oddly, her throat began to tighten and her bottom lip began to quiver. She urgently rose to her feet, packed up, and escaped into the hall, continuing on to the B hall girls room.

She pushed past the crowd of girls, through a cloud of cigarette smoke, entered a stall, and locked the door behind her. She pressed her back against the door and silently began to sob. Cynde wasn't sure why she felt so guilty. Becky had betrayed her, had exposed an antagonistic version of her darkest secret to the entire school. She had traded Cynde's friendship for an opportunity to gain social status. But for some reason, Cynde felt positively sick over the pain she'd just inflicted.

During last period, Cynde managed to score additional praise, this time from Ms. Kaminski.

"Class, I would just like to publicly acknowledge a student for her continued display of tenacity. Ms. Ehler, your improvements in this class have been nothing short of remarkable. *Truly* remarkable!" she announced. "It just goes to show what a person can accomplish when she puts her mind to it. I just want to let you know that your hard work has not gone unnoticed, Ms. Ehler. You've been doing fantastic work lately."

Much to Cynde's surprise, Ms. Kaminski's speech was followed with yet another round of cheers for her, students congratulating her work. Of course, Cynde knew it was all Justin's doing. She'd still be getting a C if he hadn't refused to accept her sloppy mistakes and forced her to completely rethink her approach to algebra.

Cynde packed up her books and stood by the door, uninterested in hearing any more from messy magenta-lipped Ms. Kaminski or the class. She waited for the bell. When it rang, she darted out the back exit of the building.

Her backpack was heavy. She knew she should have dropped most of the weight at her locker, but she couldn't face any more of the mob. Tucking her thumbs beneath the straps of her backpack in an effort to relieve some of the weight on her back, she walked around and out to the front of the building.

"Hey, Cynde!" Zach called to her. "Hop in."

Grateful, she made her way over to Zach's car.

"Hey, Zach. Thanks," she said, dropping her heavy backpack to the passenger side floor and slipping into the seat.

"No, problem. Headed home?"

"Actually, I need to go to Justin's to feed the fish. Then I'll probably just hang around there."

"Cool, cool... Actually, if you don't mind running something in for me," he said, gesturing toward his backseat, "I borrowed his jacket...like 2 months ago now. I keep forgetting to return it."

Cynde turned and saw the denim jacket on the back seat, right away noticing the Levi Strauss label inside.

Justin, my Justin...

She continued to stare at his jacket longingly another moment before picking it up to hold in her lap, running her fingers over it.

Zach smiled at her. "You miss him, huh?"

Cynde nodded, feeling her bottom lip quiver.

He's only gone for a day. Don't be such a baby.

"Well, I'm sure he misses you too," Zach said.

Cynde smiled back at Zach, holding tight to Justin's jacket. Gazing up, she noticed the small scabs on two of Zach's knuckles. There seemed to be a bit of bruising around them too. Zach noticed her staring at his hand and shifted uncomfortably in his seat.

"So, Justin says we'll be sharing a car for Spring Fling... you two, and me and Nicolette," he said cheerfully. When Cynde didn't respond, he continued, "Nicolette went with friends to pick out shoes today. Got your shoes picked out?" he asked.

"Oh, um...not yet."

"Well...still plenty of time for that," he said, pulling in front of Justin's house.

"Come inside with me?" Cynde asked.

Zach hesitated.

"I'd appreciate the company. It's weird walking into an empty house," she said.

"Sure thing," he said, smiling politely.

They got out of his car and walked up to Justin's front door. Shifting the weight of her heavy backpack to one arm, she noticed her hands were suddenly shaky, and she struggled to get the key into the lock.

"Let me help," Zach said, taking hold of the key, his hand brushing against her's.

Cynde stared at his hand. She wanted to examine the scabs and the bruising, but he quickly unlocked the door and held out his arm for her to enter. She stepped into the house, hearing Zach enter and close the door behind her. He began wandering around the living room. Cynde dropped her heavy backpack onto the floor of the alcove, then dropped Justin's jacket over the back of a tall wingback chair.

She followed Zach over to where he was standing. He was smiling up at a framed photograph on the wall. Cynde reached down and took Zach's hand, feeling his body tense immediately. She stared into his eyes as she lifted his hand, then looked down at the scabs on his knuckles. She brought her other hand up, cradling Zach's hand in hers, lightly stroking his knuckles with the tips of her fingers.

"It's nothing," he said quietly.

Cynde brought his hand to her lips and kissed his knuckles. Zach cocked his head, letting out an uneasy chuckle, and gently pulled his hand away.

"Well, I'm gonna head out now, Cynde," he said, turning to leave. "You give my best to Justin."

Cynde grabbed Zach's hand again and moved close to him, slipping her arm around his waist. She caressed his hand with her thumb, then released it and moved her hand up his abdomen, over his chest, his shoulder, and up to the nape of his neck. His body felt somehow familiar to her. She looked up into his face, his serious hazel-green eyes staring back at hers. She noticed his pronounced brow ridge was furrowed, his jaw clenched.

With the tips of her fingers, Cynde reached into his soft blonde hair and pulled his face toward hers. She noticed his faint smell, a combination of Ivory soap and maybe sawdust. She breathed him in before pressing her lips to his.

"Cynde," Zach said softly, easing his head back.

Cynde brushed her lips against his again.

"Cynde," he repeated. "I don't want to do this."

Cynde reached her hand between his legs.

"Yes, you do," she whispered, stroking him.

"Cynde, stop," he said, his voice strained. "Stop!" he repeated, pulling away.

She wrapped her arms tightly around his waist, rubbing her body into his. Zach's breathing turned rough. Suddenly, he grabbed hold of her shoulders, and spun her around, shoving her against the tall wingback chair. Alarmed, she clutched the top of the chair. Zach clamped an arm over the top of her shoulder and thrust his hip into her back, pinning her against the chair.

She heard him unbuckling his belt and soon his body began jerking rapidly. She listened as his breathing grew faster and louder as she stood, shocked, staring down at Justin's jacket. His wild, rapid movements went on for just another minute or two. Then she heard him make a noise that sounded like an angry growl—the deep primal sound of a feral beast. There was a brief pause before he pulled his arm away. Cynde felt him refastening his belt. Then he finally stepped away, freeing her.

She turned and stared at him, wide-eyed. Panting, Zach stared back with a look of rage mixed with confusion. Cynde watched in horror as his face twisted with disgust. She felt her own face crumple with shame and humiliation, hot tears spilling down her face.

"I'm sorry, Zach," she blurted. "I'm so sorry."

Zach walked toward the front door, as Cynde continued to sob. At the door, he stopped to tuck in his shirt, turning partway back.

"You don't have to be sorry, Cynde. This never happened," he said, his voice rough. "It never happened, and it never will."

He opened the door, stepped out, and closed it behind him.

As Cynde turned to leave the living room, she caught sight of the framed photograph Zach had been looking at. It was a picture of Mrs. Helvig with her arms around both boys who looked maybe 10 at the time. They were wearing winter coats, standing in the Helvig's snow-covered backyard, the three of them smiling like they'd all just heard an outrageously funny joke.

As she started toward Justin's room, Cynde could feel the wet spot on the back of her dress. She stopped in the bathroom, removed the dress, and washed it in the sink. She continued on to the bedroom where she draped the dress over the back of Justin's chair. Then, in just her underwear, she climbed into Justin's bed, burying her face in his pillow, and fell asleep.

Twenty-Six

"Hey," she heard Justin's voice say next to her ear. "Mmmm... There's a naked girl in my bed."

Cynde opened her eyes to a dark room and began turning onto her back.

"Uh-uh," Justin said, holding her still, face down. "Stay just like that."

She heard him undressing, then felt him lowering the blanket. He reached around her and she lifted herself up so he could unclasp and remove her bra. He moaned, kissing her shoulders and back, then pulled her underwear down her legs and over her feet.

He climbed onto her, laying his body over hers.

"How did I get so lucky?" he whispered.

He kissed the side of her face, gently thrusting into her.

"I missed you, Cynde," he said in her ear. "I know it's only been a day, but it felt longer."

Cynde began to cry silently into Justin's pillow. Justin continued thrusting into her, groaning against her face. He kissed her neck, then her cheek.

"Hey," he said, stopping. "Are you okay?"

She nodded, "I'm fine, Justin. Keep going."

"No," he said extricating himself. He sat up and pulled her onto his lap. "Did I hurt you?"

"No, I'm fine."

"You're not fine. You're crying. Cynde, talk to me."

"I just missed you," she said. "Sometimes when you're gone, I don't think straight. Everything just feels so overwhelming."

"Everything, like what?"

"Everything...just everything. I wish you were with me all the time."

Cynde sobbed loudly.

"Aw, Cynde…" he said, holding her. "This can't be just because I was gone for the day. What is this about?"

"I forgot to feed the angelfish!" she cried.

"You what?" he asked. "The fish? Okay. I'll go feed the fish. No biggie."

Justin lifted Cynde off his lap, setting her aside on the bed. He threw on his bathrobe and left the bedroom. After a minute, he returned.

"The fish are fine. They didn't even notice," he said. "Okay? Is that it?"

She nodded, sniffling. Justin smiled at her.

"You're sure?"

"I'm sure."

"How was the rest of your day? What did you do?"

"I drew a mean picture of Fat Becky. Everyone laughed at her," Cynde said sorrowfully. "Then Ms. Kaminski announced that I display tenacity in her class."

"Okay? Well, I think maybe Becky deserved the shot. And isn't displaying tenacity a good thing?"

"It's your tenacity she's talking about," Cynde said quietly.

Justin rested beside her, pulling her against him. His robe was soft and warm on her bare back.

"Cynde, I've just been pushing you to do your best. It's all your hard work that Ms. Kaminski's been noticing," he said. "You're a smart girl. You don't always get it right the first time, but you're getting stronger."

Cynde didn't want to hear anymore. She reached back and pulled Justin's robe open, wiggling against him.

"Just a minute," he said. "I got you something."

Justin got off the bed, picked his hoodie up off the floor, and dug into the front pocket. He pulled out a small black velvet box, opened it, and held it out for her to see. A sterling silver head of a bull stared up at her from the soft white satin inside. In awe, Cynde inhaled sharply, reaching her fingers out to lift it from the box. It was a ring.

"Let me put it on you," he said.

She held out her finger, and he slipped it on. The fit was perfect.

"Oh, my God, Justin, it's beautiful," she gasped. "Thank you so much!"

Justin kissed her, easing her back onto the bed. He slipped out of his robe and began climbing onto her. Cynde pounced, pushing Justin onto his back, fiercely kissing him. Straddling him, she reached down, taking him into her hand and aggressively pushed herself down on him.

She rode him hard, panting, feeling the tension building, a deep, raw, throbbing need. She moved faster and faster until her hands began to shake and her vision started to blur. In her mind's eye, she could see the powerful, fearsome, ferocious, horned beast.

Twenty-Seven

"Hey, Justin. Hey, Cynde."

"Hey."

They got on line in the cafeteria. Justin stood behind Cynde, wrapping his arms around her waist.

"Heard you got called to the office this morning."

"Yeah."

"What for?"

"Skirt's too short."

"Yeah?" Justin said taking a step back to look at her wavy floral miniskirt, then closing his arms back around her again. "I don't know. Looks pretty good to me."

Cynde turned in his arms and kissed him.

"So, you never mentioned," she said. "How was Princeton?"

"Actually, I think it could be the school."

"Really?"

"Yeah, I have a pretty good feeling about it."

Cynde smiled, then suddenly felt a rush of fear come over her.

"What?" he asked.

"What?"

"What was that look?"

"What look?"

"Cynde..."

She took a deep breath. "I just hate the thought of being here without you."

"We have another full year here together," he said, "And if I go to Princeton, very little will change. I'll still see you every day."

Cynde smiled, resting her head on Justin's chest.

"By the way," he added. "I've been hearing a lot about your new art piece. Do I get to see this thing or what?"

Cynde stayed quiet.

"C'mon...you never show me your artwork," Justin said.

"You've seen my art."

"I've seen a few drawings of bulls. They're great. But I didn't even know you drew people."

Cynde shrugged. "Sometimes."

"Well, I want to see it," he said. "Show me?"

"Okay," Cynde agreed.

"After lunch?"

"After school," she said.

"Before math."

Cynde laughed. "I didn't think anything could come before math."

"You come before math," he said, kissing her.

Throughout the day, Cynde had grown more anxious about showing Justin her sketchpad. But fortunately, Ms. Kaminski hadn't assigned any homework, so she'd just be able to show him her artwork and if he didn't like it, she could take her clothes off right away.

They sat at her kitchen table, and Cynde pulled out her sketchpad. Justin reached for it and she quickly pulled it back.

"No questions. Okay?" she said. "You can see them, but I don't want to explain them."

Justin stared back a moment. "Okay, deal," he said. "No questions."

He took the sketchpad and opened it. Cynde watched his face nervously as he paged through the drawings of bulls, then found the one of Gabe. He stared at it a while before turning to a drawing of the railroad tracks, examining it carefully.

Finally, he moved on to the next piece. Cynde watched his eyes widen. It was a drawing of him, bare-chested, sleeping. He looked up at her and smiled, reaching to take her hand. The next was a semi truck with the silhouette of a bulky driver and Nebraska plates. He looked up at her quizzically, but then turned the page to the drawing of Fat Becky.

"Oh, my God!" he said. "I can't believe she saw this."

Cynde covered her face in her hands. Justin stood and pulled her to her feet, easing her hands down from her face, holding them down at her sides. He pressed her against the wall and kissed her.

"No more hiding from me," he said softly against her lips. "Okay? You're incredible, Cynde. This is real talent. I want to see all of it from now on."

He looked back at the sketchpad, turning to the final drawing. It was the head of a bull—the one from the ring he'd given her. Justin lifted Cynde's hand to look at the ring, tracing the sterling silver head with the tip of his finger.

She pulled him back toward her and kissed him, reaching for his pants.

"Not here," he said. "Let's go to your room."

"No," Cynde said. "Right here."

She took his pants down then pushed him back onto the chair. She removed her underwear, and straddled his lap, staring into his eyes as she began to ride.

Twenty-Eight

Justin had gone bowling with Zach on Friday night. He'd invited Cynde along, but she'd declined. Instead, she spent the evening alone, drawing and catching up on homework. Saturday morning, her phone rang. She shuffled out of bed to the kitchen.

"Hello?"

"Hey, you. Just waking up?"

"Yeah," she answered. "How was bowling?"

"Excellent," he said. "I missed you, but it was really good to catch up with Zach."

"Cool."

"So, I've got a game today at 11. Can I come see you after?"

"Baseball?"

"Uh-huh."

"Can I come watch it?"

There was a pause.

"I would actually love that," he said, sounding genuinely pleased. "Do you really want to come watch?"

"Yeah. Where is it?"

"Home game," he said. "The island."

"I'll be there."

"Wow," he said. "My girl's coming to watch me play baseball."

"Is that weird?"

"No, not at all," he said. "It's wonderful. I just hope you're not bored."

Cynde showered and dressed in her patchwork minidress. She brushed her hair into pigtails, smoothed on her cherry lip gloss, laced up her combat boots, and headed to the kitchen. Her mother was seated at the table with a cup of coffee.

"Hey, babes," she said. "Come sit with me."

"I can't. I gotta go."

"Where ya headed?"

"Justin's baseball game."

"You want braids?"

Cynde looked at the clock.

"I'll do your hair then drive you to the field. How's that?"

"Okay," she said.

Cynde went to her bedroom and sat on the bed. Her mother followed, standing at the corner, french braiding Cynde's hair.

"So, your birthday is coming up."

"Yeah," Cynde replied.

"Saturday."

"Yeah."

"Sweet 16!"

"Okay."

"Well, I was thinking I could take you out to dinner... someplace nice, like Le Bec-Fin?"

Le Big-Fag... ooh la la

"Actually, Spring Fling is the night before, so I might be all partied out by Saturday."

"Oh! We better hurry and get you a dress!"

"I already have the dress."

"Really?"

"Yeah. Justin's mom picked it out. It's getting tailored."

"Oh," her mother said, sounding disappointed. "Well, what about shoes? We could go shoe shopping."

"I don't know... Kinda thinking I'd just wear my boots."

"You girls today sure know how to make a statement," she said.

"It's a floor-length dress. No one's really gonna see anyway."

"Well, I like it," she said decidedly. "Be who you are. To hell with tradition!" She began french braiding the second pigtail. "Anyway, I was thinking Saturday morning, we should head over to the DMV. I picked up a driver's manual for you to study, and the forms. I already filled out mine. And I got you a doctor's appointment on Wednesday to get you the required physical."

"Hmmm," Cynde replied.

"Wednesday morning, so I'll have to pull you out of school."

"Nice."

171

"I thought you'd be more excited about getting your learner's permit. Don't you want to learn to drive?"

"I guess so," Cynde said.

She had actually already learned to drive. One evening, when she was 12, following an especially ugly argument between her parents, her father had brought Cynde to Clover, the local discount department store, to buy her a new sketchpad and pencils. They'd stopped at the snack bar, and he'd bought her a cherry Icee. Then, on the way back to the parking lot, he'd handed her the keys to his pickup truck. For years, Cynde had begged him to teach her how to drive, but he'd always insisted she wasn't ready.

"Am I really ready?" Cynde remembered asking him that night.

"Do you feel ready?" he had replied.

She'd nodded. Her father had given a single nod back before spending the next hour letting her drive around the store's parking lot and the adjacent ACME parking lot. At one point, she'd gotten overly confident and had backed his truck square into a lamppost, putting a small dent in the bumper.

"Don't worry about it," he'd said with a wink. "That's why I brought the truck."

Her father had worked for a marketing firm and had driven a shiny Cadillac to work each day. But on the weekends, he enjoyed woodworking. He had built the coffee table, end tables, all of the bookshelves in their living room, and the shelves in Cynde's bedroom. He'd used the old pickup for hauling the wood.

Cynde missed that old truck. She missed the living room full of beautiful handmade furniture. She missed the smell of wood shavings, and especially the smell of freshly cut sandalwood; the

172

sweet, warm, earthy fragrance that once filled their garage. Her mother had cleared out the garage very soon after her father had left, but Cynde still thought she could kind of smell him out there sometimes.

"Well," her mother continued, "Driving is certainly an important skill for a young woman. You need to be able to get yourself around. You don't want to have to rely on anyone."

"Yeah, yeah," Cynde said, agitated.

"So, Wednesday, okay? Doctor's appointment," her mother said. "I'll need to pick you up around 10."

"Sounds good," Cynde said.

"Great. And then, we'll still get to do something meaningful on your birthday," she said with a satisfied smile. "We can do Le Bec-Fin next week."

Once her mother finished braiding, she drove Cynde to the baseball diamond at "the island," Williamson Park.

"What position does Justin play?"

"I dunno," Cynde admitted.

"Okay, well, have fun!" her mother said. "I'll be out tonight. I'll leave money for a pizza."

"Thanks, ma."

Cynde made her way to the bleachers and saw that Mr. and Mrs. Helvig were already seated there. She was surprised to see them, but then realized they probably attended all of Justin's sporting events. Mrs. Helvig waved enthusiastically. Cynde headed over to sit with them. The game had already begun. Justin was pitching.

"Cynde!" Mrs. Helvig said, "So good to see you!"

"Hi, Mrs—er um—Sabrina."

Mrs. Helvig beamed at her.

"Hi, Mr. Helvig."

"Hiya, Cynde," he responded. "Have you seen Justin pitch before?"

"No," Cynde said. "This is my first time making it to a game."

"Well, you're in for a treat," he said.

"When he was smaller, they had him playing shortstop," Mrs. Helvig told her. "That's one of the most demanding positions there is. But when he got older, bigger, they realized his real gift. He's been their ace since last season."

"Ace?" Cynde asked blankly. She knew nothing at all about baseball.

"Their best starting pitcher," Mr. Helvig cut in. "Justin knows how to pace a game like a pro," he said. "He's smart, levelheaded, and the boy's got power and great stamina."

Oh, I know it.

Mrs. Helvig began cheering along with the rest of the small crowd on the bleachers. She glanced around, recognizing a few students, including Colleen Diblin who had recently begun dating Matteo Rossi, who also played on the team. Colleen waved to her. Cynde waved back then turned her attention to Justin.

He'd just struck out a player. Another was approaching. Justin looked so beautiful in his baseball uniform. Cynde had only attended one of his football games. She'd enjoyed looking at him

174

in his football uniform too, but she and Justin had only just begun dating then, and she'd found the crowd of girls hovering around her overwhelming. They'd all seemed to want to talk to her all at once. It had been loud and hectic. The baseball crowd was much smaller and much more mellow.

She watched as Justin took a small step back and lifted his front leg, swinging his arm back. He twisted his body around, then seemed to spring off his back foot, pitching the ball forward, landing on his front foot.

"Look at that control!" Mr. Helvig exclaimed.

She watched him pitch another, then another, striking the player out. She was mesmerized by the way Justin's body moved. She wished she could watch it in slow motion.

"We're going to Barnes & Noble after the game," Mrs. Helvig said. "Maybe you and Justin would like to come with us.

"Oh, maybe. I'll ask Justin," Cynde said, but she knew there was no way they'd be going to Barnes & Noble after the game. She needed Justin naked just as soon as she could get her hands on him.

When Morrisville was batting, Mr. Helvig said, "Wait til you see this. He can hit too."

Cynde watched in amazement as the guys she regularly saw walking the halls, one after the next, went up to bat. They were guys she might have never otherwise noticed, but suddenly, they all seemed kind of special. Even the less remarkable athletes added some value. They had all come out to play as a team, and there was an obvious element of respect for one another, a certain team rapport that Cynde was witnessing for the first time.

It was nothing like what she had experienced a few years back, playing field hockey. Those girls had been just as catty and boring as any others she'd known.

Justin went up to bat. He hit the first ball.

"Look at that power!" Mr. Helvig shouted.

Justin ran to first, then second, then ran toward third, diving toward the base. He slid on his belly, crashing into Pennsbury's third baseman, knocking him over. Justin jumped to his feet and helped the third baseman up. Cynde could tell he was apologizing. The third baseman seemed to take it well, laughing and giving Justin a pat on the back

"Incredible speed!" Mr. Helvig shouted.

"Wonderful sportsmanship," Mrs. Helvig commented.

By halftime, Cynde could barely contain herself. It wasn't just that her boyfriend was a gorgeous athlete with stamina, control, power, and speed; Cynde had actually begun to enjoy the game. She'd become aware of a series of hand signals being used by both teams. Morrisville players would touch their hats, then sometimes an elbow, sometimes their chest then hips. Pennsbury players seemed to be touching their noses and ears more. There was something about the combination of physical prowess and this subtle form of communication that Cynde found extraordinarily appealing.

This is truly men being men; asserting themselves, coordinating, competing, getting a little rough at times, but still managing to be courteous. So much strength and focus and finesse...and all just to play a game in the park.

Justin turned out of the dugout and began walking toward them. The front of his uniform was dirty. The front of his hair was damp with perspiration. He was looking at Cynde, smiling at her.

This beautiful creature... He's smiling at me.

"Hey," he greeted them.

"Looking great out there, son!" Mr. Helvig said.

"Thanks, Dad."

"Oh, Justin, you're doing wonderfully. I really should be recording this one," Mrs. Helvig said.

"I'm going to have to build an addition just to house those tapes, Sabrina."

"I know, I know," Mrs. Helvig said.

"I'm gonna buy Cynde a juice," Justin said, excusing them.

He wiped his hand on his pants and held it out for her. Cynde took his hand. He felt different to her. There was a newness somehow. She realized she was feeling a little starstruck after watching him perform on the baseball diamond.

"So, what do you think?"

"It's exciting," Cynde answered.

"Really? You mean it?"

"Really."

"My parents must be talking your ear off."

"They're very proud of you."

177

"Yeah, they're sweet" he said. "So, what do you want to do after the game?"

"Well, your mother invited us to Barnes & Noble, but maybe you can get us out of that. I'd just like to go hang out at my place... in my room."

"Yeah?" he said, pulling her against him, smiling. "I'm down for that."

Twenty-Nine

Justin and Cynde made love and slept the rest of the day and night in her bed. The sky was still dark when she woke in Justin's arms to him rubbing up gently against her backside. She pretended to be asleep. He continued rubbing against her, his movement growing more steady, more determined. She felt his arms flex and tighten around her and listened to the change in his breathing.

Take it, Justin. Know that you are entitled to my body, and take it.

He stopped short, rolling onto his back, resting there. After a few minutes, he rolled back onto his side, wrapping an arm around her, lying still. Still pretending to be asleep, Cynde stretched and wiggled a bit, pushing her backside into him. Justin placed his hand on her hip and began rubbing against her again.

"Hey," he said softly. Cynde kept her eyes closed, still feigning sleep.

Take me. Don't ask permission. I am yours. Bring me to life.

She listened to his sharp, uneven breathing as he continued rubbing against her, his hand clutching her hip.

"Hey," he said again, nuzzling his face against hers, breathing heavily into her ear. He was pressed squarely against her now. Just one good shove and he'd be in. Cynde stretched, backing against him, and Justin pushed into her. Cynde groaned loudly.

"Oh, my God, Cynde, I'm sorry," he said, pulling out, rolling away to his other side. Cynde rolled over to see Justin shielding his eyes with his hand.

"Justin…"

"I'm really sorry, Cynde. That was fucked up."

"No," she said, clutching his arm.

"I like basically just raped you in your own bed."

"Justin, no," Cynde said firmly. "You can't rape me. I belong to you, and I always want you inside me."

There was a pause before Justin rolled onto his back. He stared into her eyes a moment, his face slowly lifting into a smile.

"Wow," he said. "Say that again please."

Cynde smiled back shyly. "I'm yours, Justin. I always want you."

Justin rolled on top of her.

"I want you so badly all the time," she whispered as he re-entered her.

I wish I could sleep through everything else and only become conscious for this. I want to exist only for you. I want to be your prisoner, your slave, your sex doll. I don't want to know anything else. Tell me I'm yours and keep me. Keep me locked away in darkness and only let me out for this.

"You've got me, Cynde. I love you so much."

Thirty

Monday morning. Monday morning and Justin was gone. He'd left early with his parents for California. Mrs. Helvig assured Cynde they'd be back on Friday in time to pick up her tailored dress for Spring Fling.

Cynde showered, brushed her hair into pigtails, dressed in her cream and white gingham minidress, then laced up her combat boots and walked to the mirror. Smiling at her reflection, she knew right away she wouldn't be going to school.

"Hey, darlin."

Cynde smoothed on a coat of cherry lip gloss, threw on her denim jacket, grabbed her skateboard, and left the house. It was surprisingly hot outside, so she reopened the front door, chucked the denim jacket back inside, and continued on her way.

She skated down her street, onto North Harding, then onto West Bridge St. where she immediately spotted Officer Gallo and backed into the propped open door of the laundromat. He hadn't seen her. She went back out, continuing down West Bridge, nearly all the way to Pennsylvania Ave, where she turned left, picked up her board, walking up the canal path. The sun was shining brightly. The canal sparkled. The grass looked greener than usual. There was a slight breeze. Cynde breathed in deeply. There was something out here for her today. She approached the little wooden bridge, walked partway over it, and stared down at a small flock of mallards swimming around.

Her parents had brought her here as a young child. They'd walk to Carvel, buy her a sugar cone of chocolate soft-serve ice cream with rainbow sprinkles, then continue onto the canal path, her father carrying a loaf of bread for Cynde to feed the ducks. Her mother wore her hair much longer back then, never bothering to style it. It just fell long and loose down the back of one of her old, billowy sundresses.

How had that woman changed so much in such a short time?

She could remember her parents standing close, holding hands, speaking kind words to each other. She could never have imagined what the future held for them. She could never seem to pinpoint when or why things had begun to change between them.

Leaving the bridge, she continued up the canal path a bit further, then skated down the road back to N. Pennsylvania Ave. She crossed and walked to the island, passing the baseball diamond, the playground where her father had taught her to cross the monkey bars, the community pool where she had won many races at countless swim meets, on past the stage where she'd attended concerts in the park, and through the field where she'd hunted for Easter eggs every spring of her childhood.

She climbed up the dike and walked along the towpath, staring down at the blue, sparkling water of the Delaware River. It was glorious. She looked up toward the Calhoun Street Bridge. Just before it, she saw a young man wading in the river, holding a fishing rod.

What man goes fishing on a Monday morning?

She squinted against the sun, trying to determine if it was another high school student playing hooky, but was unable to see his face. She continued walking, admiring his bare broad shoulders, strong back, and muscular arms when she finally noticed, just ahead on the towpath, a pair of purple Doc Martens.

"Seth!" she called out to the man.

He turned around. There he was. Seth Fischer.

Seth Fischer the fisherman

"Who's that?" Seth called back. "Sun's in my eyes."

"Cynde Ehler"

"Oh, hey!" he said, climbing up the rocks with his fishing rod.

Cynde stared at the wet denim clinging to his strong thighs, glancing up at his lean, bare torso, and his well-defined pectoral muscles. As her eyes continued moving over him, she noticed a faint trail of hair below his navel, wishing she could reach out and caress it with her finger. Finally, Seth reached the towpath and stood gazing at her.

"Well, look at you!" he said. "All grown up, huh?"

She smiled, admiring his face as she had done before on many occasions. He had dark brown eyes, and thick, wavy brown hair. His square jaw was almost as wide as his cheekbones, and he had elongated dimples on each cheek.

Seth had graduated from Morrisville High two years ago. He'd gone to Temple University to major in business, but Cynde had heard he'd since dropped out.

"Same purple Doc Martens?"

"The very same," he grinned.

When she was younger, Cynde used to get her mother to drive her to Fischer Books, just outside of Morrisville. Seth's great grandfather had owned the store, passing it onto his grandfather, who passed it onto Seth's father. And Seth had worked at the store all through his teenage years. He was soft-spoken and polite, but Cynde always thought he looked a little bit tough.

The summer before 8th grade, she had become an avid reader of fiction, requiring a new purchase from Fischer Books several times each week. There, she'd browse through the collection, moving around to different shelves in order to watch Seth work. At some point he'd caught on to her routine, and had begun winking at her. Initially, she'd been mortified, having been caught spying on the beautiful older boy, but she couldn't seem to stop herself from going back to the store every few days and doing it again.

One day, he finally asked her name and about all the books she'd been reading. They'd all been novels targeting dopey early adolescent girls. Cynde could tell Seth wasn't actually interested in hearing about the books. She could also tell he wasn't interested in her. Still, from that day on, he'd always made it a point to stop and say hi, to ask about her day, to be kind.

"You uh… You sure look different," Seth said. "You must be—what, 16, 17 now?"

"Yup," she said. "So whatcha doin here on a Monday?"

"Fishing."

"I can see that," Cynde said. "You catch anything?"

"Catfish. I catch 'em and throw 'em back," Seth said.

"How come?"

"Only need one. Figure if I'm gonna put in the time to clean it and cook it, I might as well wait for the right fish. Mostly just in it for sport, I guess."

"Well, it's definitely a nice day to be out on the water," she said. "You're no longer working at the bookstore?"

"I still help out there," he said.

"How's your dad?"

"Dad's the same. Quiet. Stubborn. Head in the clouds. Still thinks business is gonna pick back up any day now."

"Maybe it will," Cynde said. "It's a great store."

"Sure, sure," Seth said with a light sigh. He looked her up and down. "You wanna take a ride?"

"Okay," Cynde said.

"Truck's parked down there," he said, pointing to the bottom of the dike.

He picked up his Docs, shoved them into the crook of his arm, then offered his other arm to Cynde. Seth's skin was warm. She enjoyed the feel of his body brushing against the back of her arm as he helped her to the bottom of the dike. There, he released her arm and walked to the passenger door of his old blue and white Chevy K10, opening it for her.

She placed her skateboard on the floor and climbed onto the seat. Seth slammed the door closed, and Cynde watched him walk around to the back, admiring his strong, suntanned body. He chucked his boots into the back of the truck then reached in and took out a white t-shirt, pulling it over his head.

Seth got into the truck and started the engine. G Love & Special Sauce's "Dreamin'" came on mid-song. He turned down the volume.

"So, I don't exactly have a plan," he said. "Any place you wanna go?"

"Toad Island?"

"Toad Island," he repeated with wonder. "Are kids still going to Toad Island?"

"Oh, I don't know," Cynde said. "I haven't gone there in a long time. But it's nice and hot. Good day for a swim."

Seth smiled. "Sounds like a plan."

He drove up River Road into Yardley. Cynde liked watching Seth drive barefoot. From the corner of her eye, she watched his foot on the pedal, noticing the small patch of hair on his big toe. She looked up at his left hand on the wheel, his right arm tossed back over the blue and white bench seat. Cynde wished she could slide in close and snuggle under his arm.

It was a short drive to Toad Island. Seth pulled off the road, and they got out. Cynde walked up closer to the river. She untied and removed her boots, then her socks, setting them beside a tree, and dipped her toes into the water.

"Too cold?" Seth asked.

"I can handle it," she said.

"I don't have a towel or anything. You'll be stuck going home in a wet dress."

"Well, I guess I better take it off," she said, pulling the dress over her head and dropping it onto her boots.

She stood in her white cotton bra and underwear, smiling coyly at Seth. Seth pressed his lips together a moment then stripped down to his blue and white plaid boxers. Cynde stared longingly at his body, her eyes again landing on the faint trail of hair below his navel.

"Ready?" he asked.

186

"Ready," she said, snapping her eyes up to meet his.

Together, they waded into the water. It wasn't quite as cold as she'd initially thought. Once they'd reached beyond the shadow of the trees, the water actually felt kind of warm.

"Not too bad, huh?" Seth said.

Cynde smiled at him. The water seemed to get a little deeper than the last time she'd crossed to Toad Island, but the current felt calm enough to cross without worry.

"Y'alright?" Seth called out.

"Yup," she called back.

"Oh, that's right," he said. "You're actually quite a strong swimmer, aren't you?"

"Strong like a bull!" Cynde shouted.

"I remember now," he said. "Well, I'll stop worrying about you then."

Once they got across, Cynde began shivering. She found a nice sunny spot in the grass, sat down and hugged her knees. Seth sat beside her.

"I haven't been here in a long time," he said. "It's beautiful though."

"Yeah," she agreed. "Actually, this is my first time being here in daylight."

"Mine too," he said with a small laugh.

The last time Cynde had come out to Toad Island was a bit over a year ago when she was 14, almost 15. She'd come out with Rory Baskin, a senior at Conwell Egan, the newly coed Catholic high school in Fairless Hills following the merger of Bishop

Conwell, the former all-girls school and Bishop Egan, the former all-boys school. Rory had been something of an outcast at Conwell Egan and had taken up a friendship with Jesse Lynch, a boy Cynde only sort of knew from school. Jesse Lynch was a stoner. Rory had been one too. He'd gotten Cynde high a bunch of times. She never cared much for weed, but she'd thought Rory was cute; a bit on the skinny side, but tall with shiny shaggy hair, and he played bass in a jazz-funk fusion band. Rory would regularly spend the night at Jesse's house so he could visit Cynde and get her to sneak out of her bedroom window. That was back when her mom was still at home most nights, watching television in pink hell.

Cynde hadn't realized Rory had brought her to Toad Island that night to have sex. She'd kissed him and let him feel her up and grind against her, but when he had tried to remove her clothing, she'd stopped him, informing him she wasn't ready. Rory had been very sweet about it, insisting it didn't matter, reassuring her that he cared enough about her to wait. But soon after that night, Rory stopped calling as much and rarely spent the night at Jesse's. Cynde had been hurt by it at the time, but now just found the memory somewhat embarrassing.

"So, what's up with the bookstore?" she asked. "It used to be busy in there every day. What happened?"

"Barnes & Noble happened," Seth said. "We've seen declines ever since the one opened in Oxford Valley last year."

"Oh."

"Yeah," Seth said. "Dad's mostly in denial. Thinks it's just a matter of finding the right hook to bring his customers back."

"Maybe he's right."

188

"Nah," he said. "Once people get their heads turned, there's no going back. It's a dying game. Ya know, people are starting to buy books over the internet now? Dad doesn't even own a computer. He's holding onto nothing."

"Oh," Cynde said, suddenly feeling very sad. "Well, what'll you do?"

"I don't know," Seth said with a shrug. "Dropped out of school. I just... well, I hated it. Sitting there, listening to people say things that don't matter, things you know can't possibly be true. But I guess if you want to survive, you become one of those people who believes those things, or at least repeats them. And... well... maybe I just don't."

"Don't want to survive?"

Seth chuckled, then smiled at Cynde. "I'll survive. Just probably not here. I'm not interested in researching the best flavored coffee drinks to lure customers into a bookstore so that I can live another month."

"Where will you go?"

"I don't know," he said. "I live simply, so I've got a little money saved up. Lately, I've been thinking of moving West."

"California?"

"Nah, not that far West," he said.

"Oh," Cynde said. "Someplace like Nebraska?"

"Hmmm...maybe," he said thoughtfully, looking over at Cynde. "What do you know about Nebraska?"

"Not much, I guess," Cynde said. "But I'd like to go there."

"Really?" he asked. "What for?"

"I don't know," she said. "Maybe to milk cows and husk corn."

Seth turned to Cynde, gazing into her eyes. He stared at her silently for what felt like a long time, making her squirm a bit as she continued shivering.

"Cold?" Seth asked.

She nodded.

"Can I help you with that?" he asked.

Cynde smiled.

Seth moved in close to her, resting his fingers along her jawline, cradling her chin in his palm. She thought he was going to kiss her, but he just held her face close to his, staring into her eyes, breathing softly against her mouth.

"Huh. Little Cynde Ehler... all grown up," he said quietly.

Cynde watched his dark eyes as they searched her face another moment before he wrapped an arm around her, easing her to the ground. He climbed on top of her and finally kissed her. She kissed him back, suddenly desperate to feel him inside her. She began tugging at his damp boxers. He took hold of her wrists and held them up near her head.

"I'm not ready for that," he said softly against her lips.

"You feel ready to me," she whispered.

He pressed into her. "Yeah?"

Cynde gasped. "Uh-huh."

He kissed her lips then slowly up the side of her face and over to her ear where he nibbled her earlobe a bit.

"I like to take my time," he said quietly.

I like to take my time
I mean that when I want to do a thing
I like to take my time and do it right

He lifted his head. "Did I just hear myself quote Mister Rogers?"

Cynde laughed. Seth laughed with her.

"Anyway," he said, looking down at her. "Slowly. I like to take things slowly. I want to enjoy this."

"Okay," Cynde said with a smile.

"Okay," Seth said, releasing her wrists.

Seth did take things slowly... very slowly. Cynde was pretty sure he'd explored and kissed every inch of her body before finally taking her. He brought her to orgasm twice before pulling out and releasing onto her belly. Then, he let her nap in his arms a little before taking her again.

Afterward, it was beginning to get dark. Cynde remembered she still needed to feed the angelfish.

"We should probably swim back," she said.

"Sure you wouldn't rather just live here with me, naked on Toad Island?" Seth asked. "I'll keep you warm."

Giggling, Cynde pulled on her underwear then fastened her bra. She stood up and began wading into the water.

"Alright," he said, standing. "Back to reality. Maybe I'll talk you into coming back here with me again someday," he said, wading in beside her. "Or maybe I'll just kidnap you and drive you to Nebraska."

Cynde inhaled sharply, feeling her hands tremble a bit. She looked over at Seth, and he winked at her.

Thirty-One

Cynde exchanged numbers with Seth, tucking the small slip of paper into her bra, then asked him to drop her off at Anthony's Pizza, claiming she was meeting some friends there. She liked Seth, but didn't want to risk having him show up unexpectedly at her house, or worse, Justin's house.

Cynde carried her skateboard into Anthony's then turned to wait for Seth to pull away.

"Sit down," a voice said behind her, startling her.

She spun around.

"Zach!"

"Sit down," he repeated. "I'll buy you a slice."

"Oh. No, thanks," she said. "I actually have to go feed the angelfish."

"Sit down," Zach said again sternly, his eyes even more piercing than usual. He followed up with a polite smile as he gestured toward an empty table.

Cynde sat on the red plymold bench seat attached to a white plymold table.

"Two slices!" Zach called back toward the counter before sitting across from Cynde.

Cynde stared across the table at him, his serious hazel-green eyes studying her face. She could feel herself trembling.

"Who dropped you off just now?" he asked.

"An old friend of mine from Yardley," she said, hearing her voice shake.

"Huh," he said, watching her face.

"Zach, I should get going."

"No, stay and eat. You came into the pizza place. For what?"

"Well, I—I was going to get pizza but then realized I left my money at home."

"Two slices!" Anthony called from behind the counter. "Ah, Cynde! Cynde with the beautiful eyes! Nice to see you, doll! Tell your mother I say hello."

Cynde smiled and nodded at Anthony as Zach picked up the slices from the counter and returned to the table.

"My treat," he said, dropping a slice in front of Cynde.

She stared down at the food unsure she could manage a single bite.

"Thanks, Zach."

"So, this old friend from Yardley? What's his name?"

"Does it matter? I don't think you know him."

"Well, we've established it's a guy."

"Zach—"

"Cynde, you've got just as much on me as I've got on you," Zach said. "Maybe more since I think you know breaking Justin's heart would be much harder on me than it would be on you."

"Zach, I love Justin."

Zach's lips curved into a wry smile. "You know, I almost believe you when you say that."

"I have to go."

"Don't move," he said, keeping his voice low. "Don't even think about getting out of that seat."

Cynde stared wide-eyed, too frightened to know what to do or say.

"I actually do think you love Justin as best you can. But Justin is a guy who expects loyalty, and deserves it. It's a requirement for being close to him. And we both failed to meet that requirement. What troubles me is, if I come clean, I don't just lose the only brother I've ever known; I completely destroy him."

"Zach—"

"What troubles me more is: I don't believe that time was the first or the last time you've been disloyal to Justin. So, by remaining silent, I'm standing by and allowing him to be deceived."

Cynde could feel tears stinging her eyes, and looked away.

"Am I wrong?" he asked. "Tell me I'm wrong."

"You're wrong."

Zach's strong eyebrow ridge furrowed, his serious eyes examining her face, then staring directly into Cynde's eyes. She was sure he could see her body shaking and hear her heart racing.

"Zach, I was—I was really upset that day. I had just had a fight… with my mother, and I was missing Justin. I did something I'm not proud of. And I'm sorry. I'm really sorry, Zach."

The tension in Zach's brow eased a bit, and he gave a single nod.

"Okay. Me too. I was caught off guard and...well, needless to say, I didn't handle myself well. And I'm sorry for that, Cynde. I'm sorry too."

"Friends?" she asked reaching a trembling hand across the table.

Zach seemed hesitant, but he took her hand. She smiled as best she could then tried to lift her hand away, but he held on to it.

"I want to believe what you're telling me, Cynde. I really want to believe you. I'm gonna let go of what's happened because it best suits me, and maybe it best suits him, but I'll be watching closely. I've got absolutely nothing better to do with my time than protect Justin. Got me?"

Cynde nodded, offering another weak smile. "I really do have to go now, Zach."

"Eat your slice," he said releasing her hand.

"I'll bring it with me."

"Alright," he said. "I'll drive you."

"No, it's cool. I have my board."

"It's dark. I'm driving you," he said, his eyes focused directly on hers.

"Okay," she relented.

She stood, picked up her skateboard and the slice of pizza and walked toward the door. Zach picked up his slice, dropped some money on the counter, then walked to the door and opened it for Cynde.

Once in the car, Zach started the engine. Ween's "Piss Up A Rope" came on mid-song. He shut it off.

"Justin's?"

"Well, actually, I need to get home first."

"Home, then Justin's."

"Just home. I can make it the ten blocks to Justin's myself."

"Wherever you need to go tonight, Cynde, I'll be driving you."

Cynde sighed. "Fine, Zach. I went swimming, so I need to shower and change my clothes. If you want, you can sit and wait in pink hell."

"I'll wait," he said evenly. "Sorry, did you say 'pink hell'?"

"You'll see."

As they drove, Cynde became aware of Zach's smell: a mix of Ivory soap and what was almost certainly sawdust. The memory of that day with him came rushing back, and she felt her face flush with humiliation.

When they reached Cynde's house, Zach followed her to her door. She dropped her skateboard in the closet, picked up the denim jacket she'd tossed to the floor earlier, then dropped it with the slice of pizza on the kitchen table. They walked into the living room. Cynde tossed the fluffy pink pillows off the pink sofa and onto the pink floor.

197

"Pink hell," Zach said quietly. "Huh."

"You can turn on the TV if you want."

Cynde excused herself to her room. She showered, brushed her hair into pigtails, and dressed in her baggy overalls and a white t-shirt. She also packed clothing for school the next day since she now planned to sleep at Justin's. She certainly wasn't going to have Zach drive her back home again.

"Driving is certainly an important skill for a young woman. You need to be able to get yourself around. You don't want to have to rely on anyone."

She stepped out into the hall, then wandered to the kitchen where she found Zach examining her artwork. He was staring at her drawing of Justin.

"This is incredible, Cynde. It looks just like him. Has Justin seen this?"

She nodded.

"You've got quite a gift. I'm truly impressed."

"Thanks," Cynde said, packing her sketchpad into her backpack and throwing it onto her back.

"Ready?"

"Ready."

They walked out to his car. Zach sat quietly in the driver's seat a moment.

"I'm really glad we've managed to get past the awkwardness, Cynde. I hope you know I want to be your friend."

"I appreciate that, Zach. I also hope to be friends."

He offered a polite smile and a single nod as he started the engine.

"Am I smelling sawdust?" she asked.

"Shop class," he said, pointing his thumb toward his back seat as he drove. "Mr. Markley kinda gives me free reign."

Cynde turned and saw a few long boards of cedar along with many smaller cuts, and some stained finished wood products. She noticed a mahogany kitchen cutting board, a chess board that she thought might be beech wood, a maple jewelry box, and a smaller cherry jewelry box with an intricate hand-carved design. She reached up and clicked on the interior light. The finished pieces were flawless—perfectly smooth and meticulously stained. She was blown away.

"Oh, my God, Zach," she said in awe. "Did you make those?"

"Yep."

"They're spectacular," she said.

"Thanks," he said. "Only thing I'm really good at."

She stared back another moment, admiring Zach's beautiful work, then clicked off the light and looked at Zach.

"What about football?"

"Eh… Football is Justin's game."

"Well, I don't know anything about it, but from what I hear, you're a pretty talented player too."

Zach shrugged. "Justin's game," he repeated. "I only went out for the team in the first place so his parents would let him play."

"Really?" Cynde asked.

"Yeah. His dad was worried about injury. He still worries, but he feels better knowing I'm out on the field with him. Justin ever tell you he used to box?"

"Yeah, I actually watched a video of one of his fights."

"Heh... yeah. Sabrina likes to film every step that boy takes," Zach said, smiling brightly. "Once he got his face busted up though, that was it. No more boxing."

He parked in front of Justin's house, got out, and walked around to the passenger door. Cynde lifted her backpack and the clothes she packed, and got out.

"Let me help," Zach said, taking the backpack.

The two of them went up the front walk, where she again struggled with the keys.

"I got it," he said, taking the keys and opening the door for her.

"Thanks, Zach."

"No problem at all, Cynde. See ya tomorrow?"

"I'll be there."

"Cool, cool," he said. He lifted his index and middle fingers to his face, pointing at his eyes, then pointed at her. "I'll see ya."

Thirty-Two

Cynde bundled herself snugly in Justin's bed, breathing in deeply, but she was too anxious to take comfort in his smell; her mind and body buzzing with agitation. Suddenly, everything felt much too tight.

She threw off Justin's blanket and turned onto her side, then her other side. She thought of Nebraska… cows, corn, Seth. She thought of the way Seth had looked at her, the way he'd pressed his body to hers and held her wrists, controlling every minute as he kissed and touched her all over.

She reached a hand down in between her thighs, and her thoughts immediately shifted to a pair of serious green-flecked eyes beneath a strong furrowed brow, and the smell of Ivory soap and sawdust. She could feel the tension building inside her, the tingles in her face and the shakes in her hands.

For the last six months I've been packin' your bag
You can wash my balls with a warm wet rag
Til my balls feel smooth and soft like silk
I'm sick of your mouth and your 2% milk
And I'm no dope, but I've lost all hope
So hit the fuckin' road and piss up a rope

She gasped as her quaking body went rigid, then warm and languid. She fell asleep.

***

Tuesday morning, Cynde woke in Justin's bed. She got up, showered in his bathroom, and dressed in the clothes she had packed: her plaid mini jumper dress and a white t-shirt. The outfit

201

felt somehow wrong, but it was all she'd packed. She went into Justin's closet to see what she could find. Right away, his denim jacket caught her eye.

She took the jacket off the hanger and pressed it to her face, searching for the lingering smell of sawdust. But the jacket had been washed and smelled like everything else in Justin's closet. Cynde hung up the jacket, and closed the closet door. She brushed her hair into pigtails, smoothed on a coat of cherry lip gloss, laced up her combat boots, picked up her backpack, and started out the door.

And there was Zach, parked directly in front of Justin's house in his Lincoln Town Car.

"Hey, Cynde! Hop in!" he called out.

Cynde pressed her lips together, feeling that agitated tightness again as she walked toward Zach's car.

"Hey, Zach," she said, getting into his car.

His tape player had been rewinding. She heard it stop with a click and it began playing They Might Be Giants' "Subliminal." Cynde quietly sang along as Zach drove, grateful to be free of the obligation to make conversation. She couldn't help breathing in deeply to smell the wood she knew was in the back seat. Keeping her face glued to the passenger side window, she tucked her hands beneath her thighs.

Zach parked out front. Just as he did, Nicolette approached his car, waiting for him to get out. She wore a brown plaid miniskirt and a brown and white shirt. Her blonde hair fell softly around her shoulders, her cool blue eyes twinkling as she watched Zach get out of the car.

"Hey, babe," she greeted him.

"Hey," he said, grabbing her around her waist and kissing her cheek.

She doesn't even know what she has.

"Oh, Hey, Cynde!" Nicolette said, turning her attention. "When's Justin getting back?"

"Friday," Cynde answered.

"Cool. We're looking forward to Spring Fling!" she said, smiling brightly.

We. She already speaks for Zach.

"Oh, yeah... me too," Cynde said, wishing the bell would ring.

"What color are you wearing?"

"Um...white? Er um...I dunno, like a champagne color?"

"Oooh, pretty! I went with gold, so we'll actually complement each other nicely."

"Oh. Cool," Cynde said.

Nicolette wrapped her arm around Zach's waist, giving him a squeeze.

This is done now, right? Are we done?

Cynde uncomfortably backed toward the school.

"Oh, are you going in early?" Nicolette asked.

"Um...yeah," Cynde said. "I have to organize my locker."

"Oh, okay. See ya!" Nicolette said.

Cynde smiled and turned away.

"See ya, Cynde!" Zach called after her.

"Oh. See ya, Zach," she called back. "Thanks for the ride."

The entire morning dragged. And in between each period, she found herself running into Zach in the halls. She'd almost never seen him at school before, but now, here he was, popping up to let her know he was keeping an eye on her.

She felt smothered by him, suffocated. The tightness was intensifying.

With about 15 minutes left before lunch, she asked Mr. Krause for a pass to the bathroom, then packed up her backpack, and hurried down B hall to the payphone booth. She slunk in, pulled out a slip of paper and a quarter from her backpack, and dialed the phone.

"Hello?"

"Seth?"

"Yeah?"

"Hey, it's Cynde."

"Mmmm... Cynde. Ready for another swim already?"

"Come get me," she said.

"Now?"

"In like 15 minutes. Can you meet me on the side of the Methodist Church?"

"Uh, yeah, I can do that."

"Cool. See ya soon."

She slunk back out of the phone booth and made her way to her locker where she dropped her backpack. She moved back through B hall, into A hall, through D hall, then rushed past the gym, and made her way to the back exit.

She exited the school and ran through the back field and up the hill into the lightly wooded area in between the school and the Methodist Church. She hurried through the side of the churchyard, and onto West Maple Ave, where she waited. A few minutes later, the old blue and white Chevy K10 pulled up, and Cynde got in.

"Ditching school, are we?"

She smiled. Seth was dressed in a plain white t-shirt and jeans again, with his same old purple Doc Martens. He was dazzling.

"Where we headed?" he asked. "A little chilly for Toad Island today."

"How about the woods off of Crown Street? We can walk down by the canal."

"It gets pretty muddy back there in April," he said. "I'd be happy to bring you to my place if you think you can trust me not to lock you in and keep you tied to my bed for a week."

Cynde felt a sudden, intense throbbing between her thighs as her face flushed. Her ears seemed to be buzzing and her vision blurred. She swallowed, struggling for words.

"In Yardley?" she finally managed.

"Nah, that's where my parents live. I rent a place here in Morrisville, right on Bridge Street."

"Okay," she said.

"Okay," Seth repeated, driving off.

Seth's apartment was a small second-floor one-bedroom apartment. It was plain but clean with a tiny kitchen, unadorned white walls and beige wall-to-wall carpeting in the living room. There was a faint smell of vanilla and maybe something musty. Cynde couldn't pinpoint it. She realized she'd smelled it on Seth too. It was somehow a familiar smell. She found it very pleasant.

The living room had a heavily worn brown leather sofa, a desk with a computer, and a bunch of taped-up, labeled cardboard boxes along the wall.

"Did you just move in, or are you getting ready to move out?"

"Neither, actually," he said. "My life is just... kind of in limbo for the time being."

"Maybe you should teach your Dad how to use that thing," Cynde said.

Seth followed her line of vision. "Oh, I've offered, but Dad's basically under the impression that computers are satanic devices created to bring an end to human civilization."

Cynde laughed.

"I wasn't expecting to see you again so soon," he said softly, reaching a hand out to rest his fingers along her jawline, cradling her chin in his palm. He moved in close to her, his face only an inch from hers. "Your phone call came as quite a surprise."

"A good surprise?" she asked coyly.

Seth kissed her, then kissed her again. "A very good surprise."

He released her face and held out his hand. She took it and followed him into his bedroom. The room had more beige carpeting, another full wall of cardboard boxes, and a futon. It was otherwise empty.

"You're a futon guy, huh?"

"Hundred bucks, easy to move, and it's comfortable. Try it out," he said, gesturing toward the futon.

"Okay," Cynde said, starting to undress. Seth rushed to her and grabbed hold of her wrists, holding them behind her back.

"No way," he said softly against her lips. "You did that last time. I get to undress you this time," he said, easing her back onto the futon. He climbed over her, holding her wrists above her head, pressing his body down against hers.

He kissed her lips, then moved on to her neck. Cynde thought she might burst. She wriggled her arms free and slipped her hands beneath him, trying to unfasten his jeans.

"Stop that," he said, lifting her arms above her head again, holding them down tightly. "This is the problem," he said, brushing his lips against hers. "You seem to think you're here for a quickie, but I don't do quickies. You feel where I am right now?" he asked, pressing himself in between her thighs.

Cynde stared up at him, breathing heavily.

"Answer me," Seth said, staring back at her.

"Yes," she panted.

"Are you comfortable?" he asked, slowly grinding against her.

"Yes," she whispered.

"Good, 'cause I'm gonna be here for a while. Clothes don't come off until I'm ready. And you don't get to leave until I'm done with you," he said, kissing her again. "I don't know, Cynde, maybe you shouldn't have trusted me. Maybe I won't ever let you leave."

***

Cynde groggily lifted her head, searching the room.

"What are you looking for?" Seth asked, turning onto his side to face her.

"The clock."

"Ah," he said, reaching over her to the floor and pulling out a mustard yellow telephone from beneath the futon.

He picked up the receiver and hit a number on his speed dial. Cynde could hear the automated voice:

"At the tone, the time will be 5:11 and thirty-six seconds." *Beep*

"Shit," Cynde said.

"Late for something?"

"No, not really," she said. "What about you? Not working two days in a row?"

"I go into the bookstore at night to clean and restock, and to look over our dwindling sales."

"Oh," she said.

It made her sad to think about Fischer Books failing. Only a short time ago, it had been such a major part of the community. Mr. Fischer must feel like his whole world is closing in.

Cynde thought about her own world closing in. She was getting older, becoming a grown woman, and the expectations others had of her were mounting.

She thought of her mother wanting her to drive, to get good grades so she could go to college, start a career, become independent.

She thought of Justin…sweet, strong, beautiful, brilliant Justin. He had told her he loved her, and she knew he'd meant it. And she genuinely loved Justin, more than she'd ever loved anyone. She just couldn't seem to help falling in love a little bit with other men too.

She thought of Zach following her around the halls, around town, watching her. She felt the tightness returning to her body.

Zach the watchman

Zach the protector

Zach the woodworker

Zach the feral beast

She could never have Zach. He would always be there, and she could never have him. The tightness was becoming overwhelming.

"Hey," Seth said.

Cynde gasped at the interruption of her private thoughts.

"You okay?"

"Let's go to Nebraska, Seth" she breathed out.

"Heh."

"No, I mean it," she said. "I know this is brand new, but we've actually known each other for years. We're from the same place, and… well, I think we might understand each other. I can live simply too. I don't even need anything except a man to keep me warm. Let's just go."

Seth leaned over her a bit, examining her face, staring until she began to squirm.

"You sure do paint a pretty picture," he finally said.

"Well, don't you want to go?" she asked.

"Someday, sure," he said. "But I can't just leave Dad to keep up the store by himself."

"You said the store was dying."

"It is. It's a sinking ship," he said. "But it's my father's sinking ship. That means I go down with it."

"He can't want that for you."

Seth sighed and ran his fingers through his dark wavy hair.

"Dad knows I won't be running the store to pass on to a son of my own someday. He knows the dream is dead," he said. "But he's got to put it to rest in his own time. And I've got to be there with him when that time comes."

"But then, when will you start your own life?"

"Cynde," he said, running his hand over the side of her face, "Where is this coming from?"

"I want to start my own life now."

"Okay, but—"

210

"I want to start a life someplace fresh, with you. I like you. I can tell you like me. Why does it have to be more complicated than that?"

"Cynde," he said, taking a deep breath, "I do like you... a lot, but I can't take on something like that right now."

Cynde could feel her eyes sting with humiliation, and covered her face with her hands.

"Hey..." he said, putting his arm around her.

She pushed him off, sat up, and began dressing. He sat up beside her, resting a hand on her shoulder.

"Cynde..."

She shrugged him off, finished dressing, and pulled on her boots. Seth took hold of her arm.

"Don't leave like this," he said.

She pulled her arm from him, laced up her boots and stood to leave. Seth pulled on his boxers and jumped to his feet, taking her arm again.

"Hey. I don't want you to go," he said.

"Why should I stay? So you can fuck me for another hour?"

"Now you're talkin'."

"Let go of me, Seth," she said, pulling away from him again, walking out to the door.

"Cynde, stop!" he shouted.

"What do you want from me?" she turned and shouted back.

He moved in close, pressing her to the door with his body. "I want you to come back to bed with me," he said. "I want you to stay."

"I don't want to stay. I want to go. Why don't you want to go with me?" she sobbed.

Seth leaned in and licked a tear from her cheek, then kissed her while she cried.

"Trust me," he said. "A big part of me wants to believe this is a good idea. I'd love to just pack you into my truck and disappear with you across the country. And if it didn't mean leaving my father behind, I'd probably do it. But someday, you're gonna be glad I didn't do it."

"No, I won't," Cynde said quietly.

Seth stepped back, cradling her chin in his palm. He smiled gently.

"You're still in high school, Cynde. You've got all your choices ahead of you."

"Why do people keep pretending that's a good thing?" she asked. "I don't want choices. Doesn't that matter to anyone?"

Seth stared at her, his chest heaving as his breathing grew heavy. He grabbed her, mashing his lips against hers, kissing her hungrily. She struggled against him until he released her.

"Take me to Nebraska, Seth."

"I can't," he said tightly. He took a deep breath and stepped back from her again. "I can't," he repeated sorrowfully. "But you're gonna be fine, Cynde. I know you're gonna be fine. You're a smart girl with a bright future."

Cynde felt her eyes bulge with rage.

"What did you just call me?" her voice a hoarse whisper.

Seth's head jerked back a bit, his eyes widening.

"Fuck you, Seth."

Thirty-Three

Cynde turned out of Seth's apartment and ran down the stairs. Seth chased her to the tight first floor landing, pushing her against the door with his body.

"I'm sorry," he said next to her ear, wrapping his arms around her. "Cynde, I'm sorry. That's not what I meant. It's not what I should have said to you."

He turned her to face him, but she stared downward, unable to look at him.

"The world stopped making sense," he said. "My father is still a fairly young man, and I'm watching him check out, refusing to see what's right in front of him. I want to shake him. But how can I blame him for not being able to accept a world where everything he's worked for is being erased, a world where he doesn't fit?"

Cynde looked up at Seth. "You don't fit either," she said.

"And neither do you," Seth said, lifting his hand to cradle her chin in his palm. "You're right, Cynde. We do understand each other." He leaned in, kissing her hard. "Get back upstairs."

"I have a boyfriend, Seth," Cynde said.

"Yeah?"

"Yeah. He's really smart, and he's really nice."

"He's not what you need. If he were, you wouldn't be here."

Cynde looked into Seth's eyes. They were filled with heat, staring at her intensely.

"Get back upstairs," he repeated.

She remained still. "Do you know what I need, Seth?" she asked quietly.

"You need a man to keep you warm," he said, pushing against her again, "...a man who knows to stay on top of you."

In a sudden motion, he swung her around, easing her backwards onto the stairs, leaning over her. Cynde inhaled sharply.

"You don't want choices," Seth said, "So I'm only gonna give you this one: Get back in my bed, or this is gonna happen right here on the stairs."

Cynde could hear the buzzing in her ears. Her hands began to shake, and her vision blurred. She stared up at Seth as he continued staring back. Finally, she climbed to her feet. He turned her around, wrapped his hands around her upper arms, and began steering her up the stairs.

Thirty-Four

"At the tone, the time will be 9:22 and thirty-seven seconds." *Beep*

The automated voice from the phone woke Cynde. Seth had gotten up from the futon and was dressing in the dark room.

"Hey," he said. "Get dressed."

She sat up, still disoriented.

"What?"

"I want you to come with me."

"Come with you where?"

"To the bookstore."

"Why?"

"What do you mean 'why'? It's a beautiful place, a beautiful dream. Come say hi to the man fighting to keep it alive."

"Okay," she said.

It had been a few years since she'd seen Mr. Fischer, but she remembered him fondly. He'd been soft-spoken, polite, and friendly just as Seth had always been. He used to marvel over the number of books Cynde purchased.

Seth and Cynde got into his truck. He pulled her across the bench seat and draped his strong arm over her. She snuggled into him, enjoying his warmth and his smell.

It was a short drive to Fischer Books. By the time they'd arrived, the store was closed and locked. Seth unlocked the door and ushered her into the front room of the store.

"That smell!" she exclaimed. "I'd forgotten. It's this place. Your clothes and your apartment smell like it too. It's like vanilla and... I don't know... paper, I guess... something else."

"Bibliosmia," Seth said, grinning at her.

"What?"

"The smell of old books," he said. "Most older books from around 1845 on contain a lot of this polymer called lignin. It helps bind cellulose fibers together. There's a lot of lignin in paper that's made of wood pulp, and as it breaks down, it produces acids that degrade the paper, releasing volatile organic compounds."

"Oh."

"Probably more of an explanation than you wanted, but you're right about the smell of vanilla. One of the key compounds is vanillin, which adds a sweet, woody smell, very similar to vanilla."

Cynde closed her eyes and breathed in deeply. "It's more than the vanilla smell though. What else?"

"There's also toluene, which gives off a chemical smell that's kind of like gasoline, and furfural, which a lot of people think smells like almonds or almond bread," he said. "It's funny, I never really noticed the smell until after I'd gone off to college. When I came back, I finally realized what our customers were smelling. People seem to love it or hate it. To me, it's just the smell of home."

Cynde breathed in deeply again. "Oh...I *love* it."

Seth cocked his head, searching her face with his dark eyes. He reached his hand out to cradle her chin in his palm, then moved in to kiss her. He pulled his head back a bit and continued examining her face another moment, then kissed her again.

"I'm glad," he said, kissing her once more before releasing her chin and holding out his hand. "C'mon."

She took his hand. Except for the front of the store, which was wide and spacious, the store was constructed of a series of long, narrow rooms filled from floor to ceiling with books, additional shelves standing at the center of each room.

Cynde remembered scurrying from room to room, hiding behind the shelves, to watch the beautiful older boy in the purple Doc Martens as he worked. All of the books she'd purchased were shelved in the first and second rooms with all of the other contemporary books, but she'd made herself familiar with the entire store following Seth around. Now, here she was, holding his hand. It somehow felt a little magical.

Seth led her back to the office, which was off to the side of the very last room in the store. He opened the door. The office was quite large with only a single desk at the center of the room. Mr. Fischer sat, reading from a clipboard.

"Hey, Dad."

"Seth!" Mr. Fischer said, getting up from the desk covered in piles of books and papers. Mr. Fischer was built strong like Seth, and also had a head full of thick, wavy hair, most of it now silver. He wore a thick mostly silver beard over his wide, square jaw. "It's early for you. Oh! You brought a friend."

"Dad, you remember—"

"Little Cynde Ehler?!" he asked, astonished.

Seth smiled as Mr. Fischer approached her.

"Of course! No one else has eyes like those... except for your mother."

"Hi, Mr. Fischer," Cynde said, smiling at him.

"Look at you! All grown up," he said. "You used to be in here three times a week! You read all those silly girl books."

"Yeah," Cynde said with a laugh.

"I guess you're no longer a silly girl," he said.

"I mostly still am," she said.

"Well, good," he said. "The world certainly needs more silly girls."

He looked to Seth. "How's she treat you, son?"

"Very well, Dad."

"Good," he said, looking back to Cynde. "Be good to my boy. You won't find another like him."

Mr. Fischer touched Seth's face as he passed them.

"Well...I'll be heading home to your mother then."

"Give her my love," Seth said.

"Give it to her yourself. Why don't the two of you come for dinner Sunday?"

"That sounds good, Dad," Seth said. "We'll speak tomorrow."

"Okay, son," Mr. Fischer said. "Little Cynde Ehler...not so little anymore...it was wonderful to see you again, my dear."

"Wonderful seeing you too, Mr. Fischer."

"Good night," Mr. Fischer said, walking toward the front of the store.

"Good night," Seth and Cynde responded in unison.

"It shouldn't take me long to look over the sales," Seth said. "I mostly just have to clean up and straighten the shelves."

"Can I help?" Cynde asked.

"Sure," he said. "Most of the cleaning supplies are behind the counter. It's all pretty self-explanatory. You want to start up front? I'll only need a few minutes in the office."

"I'll be up front," she said, turning.

Seth grabbed her around her waist, turning her around. He kissed her then released her. She smiled at him and again turned around. Again, Seth grabbed her around her waist, turning her, this time backing her against the side of a bookshelf. He pressed against her, kissing her deeply, one hand closing firmly around her shoulder, the other over the nape of her neck. Finally, he released her again.

"Okay," Seth said, turning toward the office.

***

Cynde woke early the next morning in Seth's bed. She looked over at Seth sleeping beside her, examining the sharp angles of his face, wishing she had her sketchpad with her.

She thought of him in the bookstore. Once he had finished reviewing their sales, she'd watched as he lovingly cleaned and organized the shelves. Cynde had followed his lead, running a feather duster over every surface to clear away invisible dust, spraying and wiping the storefront window, sweeping the hardwood floors, vacuuming the Persian area rugs.

She thought of the smell.

Bibliosmia. Seth's smell. His father's smell. *"...the smell of home."*

Had she really asked him to leave it?

"...a beautiful place, a beautiful dream"

"...a sinking ship"

"...a dying game"

Could they really let such a place die?

Thirty-Five

Seth had been sleeping so peacefully that Cynde decided to slip out without waking him. She walked home to find her mother sitting at the kitchen table.

"Cynde...a note, please? Just leave a note if you're going to be out all night."

"Sorry, ma."

"Okay. Go shower. I'll braid your hair for school. Is Justin coming to get you?"

"Um, no... walking today."

"Oh. You're not fighting are you?"

"No, ma. Not fighting. I'm gonna get in the shower."

She showered and dressed in her black velvet swing dress, adding her plastic tattoo choker, applying a coat of cherry lip gloss, then pulling on her socks and combat boots. Her mother entered and began brushing and french braiding her hair in pigtails.

"Ma, remember Fischer Books?"

"Of course I remember Fischer Books. You had me driving you there two, three, sometimes four times a week. You were reading all those ridiculous adolescent romance novels. I couldn't interest you in any reasonable literature at all. And you had such a crush on that Fischer boy."

"Seth."

"Right! Seth Fischer."

"How come you don't go there anymore?"

"Oh, I don't know. I guess I've started going to Barnes & Noble. You know, they have such a big selection, and anything they don't have, they'll order, and it comes in right away. Plus, they have all that cozy seating everywhere, and that nice little cafe," she said. "Why?"

"Well, it just seems sad is all. Fischer Books served the community for multiple generations, and now they've been abandoned for some big corporation. The people who own Barnes & Noble don't even know us. They're not from here. They're not part of our community."

"Maybe not, but they seem to know what people want."

"Yeah," Cynde said. "I dunno. Just seems sad."

"Yes, I guess it is sad," her mother agreed. "Well, they're having a baby shower next week for Sheila at the office, and I still need to buy a gift. Maybe I'll stop in and check out Fischer's children's books."

"Cool. Thanks, ma. The children's section is in the second room on the left."

Her mother stared at her a moment in the mirror.

"Have you seen Seth lately?"

"Yeah, Seth's around."

"That's not why Justin isn't driving you to school today, is it?"

"No, ma. Justin is in California touring Stanford's campus with his parents."

"Oh. Stanford. That's wonderful. You know, if you really start applying yourself, you might be able to go to a school like that."

"Uh-huh," Cynde said.

When her mother finished her braids, she grabbed her denim jacket. As she headed out the door, her mother called out to her:

"Don't forget: I'm picking you up for your physical at 10!"

She hadn't reached the end of her front walk when Zach pulled up in his car.

"Hop in."

Cynde took a deep breath and got into Zach's car.

"So, you gave me the slip yesterday," he began. "And I know you were out most of the night, Cynde... maybe all of it. You wanna tell me where you were?"

"Zach, I'm breaking up with Justin."

Zach's eyes widened.

"I'm not what he needs. You know that," she said quietly. "And he isn't what I need."

Zach looked at her, "Well, I can't disagree with you, Cynde, but... I've gotta ask: Who's better than Justin?"

"No one," she said. "No one is better than Justin. I'm lucky to have ever even caught his eye. But he doesn't belong with me. And I don't belong with him."

Zach nodded slowly. "So...you want me to tell him about —?"

"No," Cynde said firmly. "No. It never happened, Zach. If you tell him it did, you're just being selfish, trying to ease your own conscience. You'd be taking everything from him."

Zach ran his hands over his face.

"It never happened," Cynde repeated. "You just tell him you caught me with some other guy... someone you don't know... which is what you'd have found if you'd known where to look," she said unflinchingly. "Make him hate me, Zach."

"I don't think he could ever hate you, Cynde."

Cynde felt tears sting her eyes. "Well, do your best."

Zach swallowed and gave a single nod.

"Thank you, Zach."

He pulled out, and they drove in silence. After he parked in front of the school, he turned to Cynde.

"Hey, Cynde," he said. "I feel weird saying this, but... Thank you."

She offered a smile and handed Zach her copy of the Helvigs' house key.

"Be sure to feed the angelfish."

Thirty-Six

As soon as Cynde entered, Ms. Ranelli, the receptionist called out to her.

"Cynde Ehler, I need to see you."

Cynde stepped into the front office. Ms. Ranelli was a short, heavyset woman with cropped bleached blonde hair. After divorcing her husband, Ms. Ranelli had begun working in the office, *"to help keep my daughter anchored,"* Cynde had once overheard her telling Ms. Mouflon, the school's disciplinarian.

Ms. Ranelli's daughter, Emilia, was in Cynde's grade. She was a quiet, chubby girl who just kept getting chubbier. Cynde wasn't sure what Ms. Ranelli was worried about since Emilia seemed to be doing a bang-up job keeping herself anchored all on her own. Girls like Emilia never got into trouble.

"You were seen leaving the school just before noon yesterday," Ms. Ranelli said. Her voice was almost as nasal as Ms. Kaminski's. It made Cynde shudder. "I'm sorry, but with all your previous transgressions on record, I have to send you home with a three-day suspension."

"Can I go get my books from my locker?"

"I'm sorry," Ms Ranelli repeated, "I can't even let you into the halls. I did talk to Ms. Mouflon though. You will still be allowed to attend Spring Fling on Friday night," she said with a note of disapproval.

Emilia hadn't been asked to Spring Fling. Girls like Emilia never got asked.

Cynde left the building wondering how many transgressions it would take to get permanently expelled. She walked home to find her mother still there, sitting in pink hell, watching television. She clicked off the TV as Cynde entered.

"What are you doing home?"

"Got suspended," Cynde announced.

"For what? You just got there."

"Got caught skipping yesterday."

"Cynde!" her mother said with a scowl. "It's like you want to fail at life. Is that what you want? Do you want to fail at life?"

"No."

"Then what?" she asked. "Is high school really so bad that you can't even show up for it?"

"Yes," she said, bored with the conversation. "Ma, can we bake?"

"What?"

"Remember when we baked all those lemon squares?"

Her mother looked puzzled for a moment before visibly recollecting, "Oh, yeah. Oh, my goodness, that was years ago. We baked dozens of them. What ever did we do that for?"

"Bake sale to support the swim team."

"Oh, right," she said. "What on Earth made you think of that now?"

"I dunno. Just feel like baking."

"Well, we have your doctor's appointment today."

"I don't want to go," Cynde said. "Let's bake lemon squares instead."

"You need to have the physical exam before we go to the DMV, Cynde."

"Well, I don't want to go there either."

"I took the morning off from work for this. I don't understand. What almost-16-year-old girl doesn't want to drive?!" her mother asked, exasperated.

"I'm just not ready," Cynde said quietly.

Her mother stared at her. Cynde stared back.

Her mother sighed loudly, pressing the palm of her hand to her forehead.

"I'll see if I can find the recipe and run to the Acme to buy you the ingredients," she said. "You do the baking. My baking days are long over."

***

Cynde had looked over the recipe and made a shopping list for her mother. After her mother left for the store, she folded and bagged up all of Justin's clothing and set the bag on her bed. Once her mother returned with the groceries, Cynde spent the morning mixing shortbread crust for lemon squares.

By 11, her mother was dressed and ready for work. She stopped at the front door.

"Cynde, I know my lecturing never does any good. I just need to stress again how important it is for a woman to give herself plenty of options," she said. "You don't want to limit yourself. Really, really, really, babes... You don't want to suddenly find yourself stuck."

"How do I zest a lemon?" Cynde asked, looking up from the recipe.

Her mother sighed. "The fine side of the grater. Just the peel. Avoid the pith. It's bitter."

Cynde's mind suddenly flashed to her father, teaching her about woodworking, sawing a piece of maple in the garage.

"Avoid the pith. It's soft and weak."

"Do we have a grater?"

"I don't know," her mother said with a shrug. "Probably somewhere."

***

Once the lemon squares had fully cooled, Cynde cut them, placing each square onto a cupcake foil, then into a plastic Ziploc bag. She stored them in the freezer, then repeated the recipe.

At 3:30, the phone began ringing incessantly. Feeling unprepared for the conversations ahead, she unplugged it and continued baking. Around 4:00, there was a knock at the door. She peaked around the living room curtain and saw Zach standing at the door, holding her backpack. She opened the door.

"Three-day vacation, huh?"

"How did you get my locker combination?" she asked, taking her backpack from him.

"Justin."

Cynde froze. "You didn't tell him."

"No, I told him."

Confused, she opened the door wider. "Come inside?"

When Zach hesitated, Cynde held up her hands in from of her.

"Just to talk," she promised.

Zach looked embarrassed but entered the house. Cynde dropped her backpack on the floor since the kitchen table was cluttered with baking equipment.

"Wow, it smells great in here."

"You told him what I told you to tell him?" Cynde asked sitting at the table.

"I did," Zach said, sitting in the other chair. "He was pretty wrecked, but when he heard you got suspended, he told me to make sure you had all your books, and to get your assignments from your teachers. So, I did. It's all in there," he said, gesturing to the backpack.

"Thanks," Cynde said, feeling very sad.

Justin…

"He seemed more pissed at me," Zach said.

"What? You didn't—"

"No, I didn't tell him. I told him what you wanted me to tell him. He said something about you losing your mind over him leaving, and that I shouldn't have been tailing you," Zach said glumly.

Cynde looked down at her lap.

"So, I'm done hassling you, whatever happens," he said, standing up from the table. "Always knew he was crazy about you."

231

Cynde looked up. "Thanks, Zach… for bringing all my stuff."

"Sure thing," he said.

"Oh, just a minute," she said, getting up and hurrying into her bedroom. She grabbed the bag of Justin's clothing, then hurried back and handed them to Zach.

"Please return these to Justin."

"Sure thing," he said again, carrying the bag toward the door.

"Take some lemon squares," she said.

"No, thanks, Cynde," Zach said, turning to leave. "I'm good."

Cynde finished baking, cooling, and packaging the lemon squares. She thought of Justin getting that call from Zach and still wanting her books and school work brought to her. She ached for him. Allowing her tears to flow freely, she cleaned the kitchen and washed all the equipment. By the time she was finished, it was nearly 8 PM.

Almost time to get to the bookstore.

Thirty-Seven

Balancing the box of lemon squares, Cynde rang the doorbell for the second floor apartment. Seth soon opened the door. He was dressed in another plain white t-shirt and jeans.

"Where have you been?" he asked, opening the door wider.

"Hi," she said, standing on his doorstep, admiring him.

"Get in here," he said, taking the box from her. "What's this?"

"Lemon squares," she said, starting up the stairs.

"A lot of them, huh?"

He followed her up and set the box on the small table in his tiny kitchen. He turned, and leaned on the counter, holding his arms open for her. She pressed herself against him, wrapping her arms around his waist. He folded his arms over her tightly.

"Why did you run out like that this morning?" he asked.

"What? Oh. Well, I had to go to school. I just didn't want to wake you."

"I would've driven you, Cynde," he said. "Next time, wake me. Don't just leave."

"I'm sorry," she said. "I'll wake you next time."

Seth eased his head back and kissed her, moving one hand down to cup her backside and the other up to the nape of her neck, pressing her into him. After a few minutes, he moved his other hand down to cup her backside too.

"Mmmm...you smell so good," she whispered against him.

"C'mon," he said, pulling her toward his bedroom.

"But it's almost time to get to the bookstore," she said.

"Not until I'm done with you."

***

Cynde rolled over, opening her eyes to the dark room.

"How can you stand not having a clock in here?" she asked.

"Just used to it, I guess," he said, dialing.

"At the tone, the time will be 11:42 and sixteen seconds." *Beep*

"We have to get to the bookstore!" Cynde said, sitting up.

"Easy," Seth said, pressing her onto her back. "I have all night for that. Anyway, I want you to stay here and get some sleep. You've got school in the morning."

"Nope," Cynde said. "Off for the rest of the week. Suspended."

"Mmmm..." he said, climbing atop her. "Sounds like Ms. Mouflon isn't able to keep you in line. Guess I'll have to do it." He began kissing her neck.

"You think you can?"

He looked up, directly into her eyes. "Do you doubt me?"

Cynde shook her head. Seth returned to her neck.

"Seth."

"Hm?"

"I was thinking."

"About?"

"About the bookstore."

"What about the bookstore?" he said looking up at her.

"Well, what if you put some comfortable chairs in there? I mean, there's plenty of space for it. Just a few chairs like in the corners of some of the rooms."

"Hm."

"And maybe you could sell coffee. It wouldn't have to be like specialty coffee or anything. Just coffee...and baked goods."

"Baked goods?"

"Yeah, like lemon squares."

He stared down at her a moment.

"Did you bake lemon squares for the store?"

"Well, I just thought you could give them away to customers tomorrow to see if people like them.

Seth kissed her hard, plunging his tongue into her mouth again and again. He moved down to her neck again.

"You're so sweet, Cynde," he moaned into her ear.

"I had one other idea though, Seth," she said quietly.

"Oh, yeah? Let me hear it," he said, cocking his head, gazing at her.

"Well, maybe you could start a website for the store."

Seth took a deep breath and noisily blew air out through his lips.

"You know what?" he said. "I did."

235

"You did?"

"Uh-huh. I built the website. It's ready to go. It's just that… Dad…"

"I know," she said. "Some old guys still practice the old ways of their grandpas, and they've got their arguments for why the old ways are superior."

"Heh. Yeah."

"A lot of their arguments are pretty good too. It's just that… well, that office is pretty big, Seth," she said, looking into his eyes. "Maybe it's time to set up a second desk in there. I mean…it's not just *his* dream, is it?"

"It's not, no," Seth said quietly. He took a deep breath and let it out shakily.

"I'm sorry," she said quickly, casting her eyes to the ceiling.

"There's nothing at all for you to be sorry about, Cynde," he said firmly, holding her face, stroking her cheek with his thumb. "I'm really touched that you've put so much thought into this. I guess I'm just now realizing that… I've accepted defeat before even putting up a fight," he said, running a hand over his face. "I've been a coward."

"A coward would have run away. You stayed. I just think there's more we could be doing."

"We?"

"Well, I just like being there with you, Seth. So, I thought maybe you could start running the online business, and I could take over the cleaning."

Seth took hold of her lips with his. Without warning, he thrust forward into her. Cynde let out a short, high-pitched shriek against Seth's mouth, shocked by the sudden invasion. He reached down and cupped her backside with one hand. Wrapping his other arm around her tightly, he squeezed her body against his, soon rocking her entire torso up and down with him as he moved, taking full possession of her.

***

It was early morning by the time they'd gotten to the bookstore. Together, they cleaned and organized the store. Cynde set up a small table of lemon squares near the register.

"Is this okay?" she asked. "What will your dad think?"

"I'm gonna drive you home now, Cynde. You need to rest, and I'm gonna have a talk with Dad. I'll pick you up later, okay?"

"Okay."

Cynde directed Seth to her house. Before letting her out, he pulled her close to him, cradling her chin in the palm of his hand, staring at her face.

"Are you nervous?" she asked.

"About kissing you? I don't know, should I be?"

Cynde giggled. Seth kissed her.

"No, this is good," he said. "I need to move slowly with Dad though. Coffee, chairs, lemon squares... I think he'll like those ideas. But that might have to be enough for today."

Cynde nodded.

"Call me later when you're ready for me," Seth said.

He kissed her again before releasing her chin.

"Thank you, Cynde. I'll see ya later."

Thirty-Eight

Cynde unplugged the phone and went directly to bed, falling asleep almost immediately. She woke around 2 PM, showered, and dressed in a white tank top and baggy overalls. Then, imagining Seth undressing her, she reconsidered, trading the overalls for a black corduroy button-down miniskirt. She pulled her hair into pigtails, then decided to take out her sketchpad. As she did, she caught a glimpse of her algebra book, and felt her bottom lip quiver a bit.

She sat at the kitchen table, sketching the box grater still sitting out, drawing the wide course surface grater front panel, and the smaller fine surface grater side panel.

"You're a smart girl. You don't always get it right the first time, but you're getting stronger."

After packing up her sketchpad, she dialed the phone.

"Hello?"

"How'd it go?"

"I was hoping it was you," Seth said. "I'm gonna come get you."

"Okay."

He arrived shortly.

"So, how'd it go with your dad?" Cynde asked climbing into Seth's truck.

"Get over here," he said, pulling her across the bench. He tucked her beneath his arm, kissing her. "It went really well."

"Really?"

"Really."

"Did he give out the lemon squares?"

"He did," Seth said. "They're a big hit."

"What about the rest... coffee, chairs?"

"He's already got my mother reupholstering some old chairs from the attic. It's a go. He said he was thrilled to have me take some initiative. Of course, it's your initiative he's talking about."

"Did you mention the website?"

"I did," he said. "He doesn't feel great about it, but he wasn't as upset as I thought he'd be. Said he thinks it's time I start to take the reins even if he doesn't agree with my approach."

Once they arrived at Seth's apartment, he took Cynde's hand, leading her up the stairs and directly back to his bedroom. He eased her onto the futon and rested beside her, propping himself on an elbow. He leaned over her, running his hand along the side of her face, sweeping his thumb across her cheekbone. Cynde snuggled into him.

"Seth?"

"Yeah?"

"What if the store started offering space to local authors and local poets, maybe even local musicians? Maybe people want a place to help promote their work."

"Huh. Yeah. I bet that could work," he said, reaching into her hair, pulling out one of the elastics, and playing with the long tresses.

He nuzzled her face then moved onto his back, pulling her close. He rested quietly a few moments.

"It'll likely fail, you know," he said. "The store. No matter what we do, it'll always be an outdated model. It's just not what people want."

"It's what they need though," Cynde said.

"Yeah," Seth said. "But they won't figure that out until it's long gone."

"Maybe they will, Seth. Maybe we can show them what's at stake before it's too late."

"It'll take some kind of miracle," he said.

"You were right though, Seth. It's a beautiful place, a beautiful dream. It's worth fighting to keep it alive for however long we can. I'm sorry I asked you to leave it."

Seth rolled her onto her back. As he began kissing her, Cynde felt him reach to the floor. He lifted her arm above her head, and she could feel him strapping something to her wrist. When he lifted his face away from hers, she looked up and found that he'd strapped a pink resin watch onto her wrist.

"It's got a light," he said, pressing a tiny button on the side of the watch which illuminated the face. "Now you don't have to wait for me to dial the phone for the time."

She brought her wrist down to examine the watch. The face of it had a picture of a black and white spotted cow on it.

"I think your dream is beautiful too, Cynde," he said. "I'm sorry I can't give you cows and cornfields now. But... maybe someday."

Cynde felt her throat tighten. She smiled at Seth as tears spilled from the outer corners of her eyes. Kissing her, he climbed on top of her.

***

Cynde opened her eyes to the dark room and pressed the tiny button on the side of her watch. It was nearly 8 PM.

Almost time to get to the bookstore.

Seth had gone to the living room. Cynde dressed, retied her pigtails, and wandered in after him to find him dressed in his usual jeans and white t-shirt, sitting at the computer. She walked over and sat on his lap. He wrapped his left arm around her, keeping his right hand on the mouse.

"You wanna see it?" he asked.

"Yeah."

He clicked a few times and up came the website, a mostly blue and white design. It said *Fischer Books, since 1923*, displaying their address, phone number, and fax number. Below, there were options for searching and ordering books. Cynde thought it was perfect—simple but elegant.

"It's beautiful, Seth," she said.

"Thank you," he said, clicking a few more times. "And... we're live!"

Together, they stared at the website.

Seth reached into her hair, pulling the elastics out one at a time.

"I don't like these," he said. "Wear your hair down for me."

She turned to look at him, blinking. He looked back.

242

"Okay," she said.

He pulled her back against him, bending to kiss her neck. She moaned and he began moving her against him, cupping her breasts, then unbuttoning the front of her miniskirt.

"I want you," he said. "Get back in bed."

"No," she said, turning to straddle him. "Right here."

Seth stared at her a moment, holding her face close to his, then stood. He turned Cynde back around, bending her over the desk, gripping her hair. She heard him opening his jeans, then felt him pulling down her underwear.

Thirty-Nine

Seth and Cynde had cleaned the bookstore and set up a casual presentation for Mr. Fischer, including ideas to engage the community more. By the time they'd finished brainstorming, the sky was light. Seth drove her to the grocery store to purchase more baking ingredients, then home.

"Don't start baking until you've gotten some sleep, okay?" he said. "I'm gonna go talk to Dad, then I'll go home and sleep too. Call me later when you're ready for me."

"Okay," she said, kissing him goodbye.

He pulled her in close.

"I never imagined a woman like you, who's willing to fight with me in what's sure to be a losing battle."

"Stop assuming we'll lose," Cynde said. "If we want people to believe, we need to believe first."

"You're right," Seth said, his brow furrowing. "I just don't want you getting crushed by this."

"I'm stronger than you think, Seth."

"I know," he said. "...like a bull."

Cynde looked down. Seth pulled her close and kissed her again.

"See ya later," he said.

Cynde nodded, smiling as she climbed out of his truck. She carried the bags of groceries into the house and set them down in the kitchen. Then, she walked back to her bedroom, got into bed, and fell asleep right away.

It was nearly 4 PM when she woke. She showered, combed her hair, and dressed in sweatpants and a t-shirt, then went to the kitchen to set up for baking. As she finished mixing the shortbread, there was a knock at the door. Cynde went to peak around the pink curtains and saw Mrs. Helvig holding a large white box.

Mrs. Helvig saw Cynde peaking out. She smiled and waved at Cynde, who took a deep breath and opened the front door.

"Cynde! It's so good to see you."

"Hi," Cynde said. "Is that the dress?"

"Yes! Finished just in time as promised."

"I guess you didn't hear."

"May I come inside, dear?"

"Oh, of course."

Mrs. Helvig followed Cynde into pink hell, where they sat together on the sofa.

"You and your mother must really love pink."

"Oh. Um...yeah."

"Cynde, I heard," Mrs. Helvig began.

Cynde held her breath a moment. "Heard what exactly?" she finally managed to ask.

"Well, Justin wouldn't say much, but I can tell he's upset," Mrs. Helvig said, resting her hand over Cynde's. It was the same way Justin often rested his hand over hers. "Cynde, I know this can be fixed. Justin loves you. He's not the fickle sort. When he loves, he loves completely. It doesn't go away. You just need to go to him. Whatever it is can be fixed."

"Mrs. Hel—Sabrina…" Cynde began. "I don't think I'm a good fit for Justin."

"Of course you are, dear!" Mrs. Helvig said. "You know, I wasn't much older than you when I met Justin's father. His father is the same way. He chooses a path and pursues it to the very end. A man like that can provide a very happy life."

"I know," Cynde said. "Justin is the very best sort of man there is. I just don't think I'm the person Justin needs me to be."

"Cynde, we all make mistakes. Don't let a mistake steal away your opportunity to be happy."

Cynde stared at Mrs. Helvig, her eyes beginning to tear. Mrs. Helvig handed Cynde the dress box.

"I know your love for Justin is true," she whispered. "Now, go put on this dress. Let's make sure it fits."

Cynde sat a moment longer.

"Sabrina, I—"

"Just try it on," she said. "Let's just see it."

Cynde brought the dress to her bedroom. She removed her clothing and slipped the ballgown over her head and fastened it in the back. She stood in front of her full length mirror, staring at her reflection. She looked like a wedding cake topper without the groom.

She walked back out to the living room.

"Oh! Oh, my!" Mrs. Helvig exclaimed, her eyes tearing up. "It's just perfect. You look absolutely perfect!"

She moved toward Cynde and embraced her tightly. Cynde closed her eyes and breathed in the familiar fabric softener fragrance.

Justin, my Justin…

Cynde cried in Mrs. Helvig's arms. Mrs. Helvig cried too, holding Cynde tightly.

"Sabrina, I—"

"Shhh…" Mrs. Helvig said, still holding Cynde. "Now you just go splash some cold water on your face. Maybe add just a touch of blush. And then go to Justin. I'd drive you over, but he'd say I'm interfering."

Mrs. Helvig released her.

"Don't worry about the past, dear," she said, taking Cynde's hands. "The correct path is still right in front of you."

She smiled at Cynde again before leaving.

Cynde sat still on the sofa until she noticed the light outside changing. Then, she pulled on her combat boots, laced them up, and grabbed her skateboard from the closet.

It was chilly outside, so she stepped back in and slipped into her denim jacket. Once at the sidewalk, she lifted the gown, hopped onto her board and skated down her street, speeding as fast as she could all the way to Justin's street. She tried to imagine what she would say to him, how she could begin to explain.

Could he really forgive her? Would he really still love her? As she neared his house, she saw Justin at his father's car, pulling a suitcase out of the trunk, then another one.

Quickly, Cynde ducked behind a thick oak tree to watch him, still not knowing what to say to him. He was dressed in his gray and white plaid lounge pants and a white t-shirt. Cynde closed her eyes for a moment, thinking of the last time she'd seen him wearing those clothes. She thought of him wrapping his warm arm around her in his bed, instructing her to sleep. She thought of him standing in his room, staring as she stood naked and trembling before him. She thought of him pulling off those same clothes, approaching her to take her for the very first time.

"This is what you want, Cynde?"

He had forgiven her. He had healed her. He had loved her.

Justin...

Justin pulled a duffle bag out of the trunk, threw it over his shoulder, then lifted the two suitcases and carried them back into his house. Cynde stood frozen, watching as he disappeared. Her throat began to tighten. Her eyes filled with tears. A wave of grief came over her. It was so powerful, she nearly fell to the ground. Grabbing onto the oak tree for support, she sobbed and sobbed, barely able to catch her breath.

Justin, my Justin...

Finally, she managed to steady her breathing and herself. She wiped her tears away, took a deep breath, picked up her skateboard, and walked. She walked onto N. Harding, crossed W. Palmer, and took Jefferson to West Trenton Ave. She took West Trenton all the way past Crown St., and continued walking to the

Calhoun Street Bridge. The sky had turned black, and the air had turned colder. Cynde shivered as she began walking onto the bridge.

At the center of the bridge, she stopped and stared down. The lights from the bridge reflected off the water. The Delaware River was black and shiny. It was magnificent.

"Justin, my Justin..." she said aloud. "I will always love you."

Cynde pulled the sterling silver bull ring from her finger, kissed it, then hurled it into the river. She picked up her skateboard and chucked it in after the ring. Then, she lifted her wrist, fingering the pink resin watch, and pressed the tiny light button.

7:48. Almost time to get to the bookstore.